Mothers

and

Other Strangers

Fran Hasson

Copyright ©2014 Fran Hasson
All rights reserved

ISBN – **13:978-1501055683**
ISBN – **10:1501055682**

Cover design by L. William Gibbons, graphic artist and author.

Back Cover photo by Jeanne Kowalski.

Cover painting by St. Croix artist, Gail Widmer, first exhibited at the Caribbean Art Museum, December 2014.

Acknowledgments

This is my second novel. I should have thought I could do it "all by myself." This shows how naïve I really am. I have even more people to thank this time!

Let me start with the old stand-bys: Maribeth Fischer of the Rehoboth Beach Writers Guild (RBWG) - and the students of her novel class for editing and suggestions; Jeanne Kowalski for the photo shoot; Stephanie Martin for encouragement and being interested in the progress of the story; Rosaleen Malone for editing; Frank Minni (also of RBWG) for editing, especially from a "man's point of view"; Gail Widmer for listening, offering suggestions, and creating her beautiful painting which is the cover of the book.

Now for the newbies: Patty Bennett for eagle-eye proofreading; my outstanding editing team: Joan Cooper, Billie Criswell, and Barb Shamp; Tia Fizzano for medical expertise; Mary Perkins for ideas and technical advice; the Rabbit Gnaw critique group for suggestions; L. William Gibbons for helping me to format the book, teaching me the basics of Word tools, and manipulating Gail's painting to make a gorgeous cover.

Thanks also to: the too-many-to-be-named who have commented and asked about the novel as it has been making its tortuous way from beginning to end.

Other works by Fran Hasson

Allawe

Dedicated to

all mothers

everywhere

who do their best

as best they can

BOOK ONE

Chapter 1

Happy he
With such a mother! Faith in womankind
Beats with his blood, and trust in all things high
Comes easy to him; and tho' he trip and fall,
He shall not blind his soul with clay.
Alfred Tennyson, *The Princess*

VERN LOOKED OUT at the moonlit night. Swooping down from the roof and in front of his bedroom window, an owl scared across the street to the marsh. It circled, watching and listening to the creatures below. As quickly and silently as it came, it snatched up a huddled mole and carried it off, passing directly in front of Vern. The predator seemed to wink at him as it gained altitude.

"Marla, look at this." But it was too late. The owl had disappeared before she could reach the sliding glass door to join him. "I've never seen an owl here before so up close and personal. That sucker winked at me!"

"This is spooky," Marla said. "Remember what they told us at the Nanticoke Museum?"

"You mean about owls being a harbinger of impending death?"

"They said unusual owl activity. I'd say that ten years living here with no owls on the roof and then suddenly this one popping in here is a bit unusual."

The phone rang, startling them. Since it was rare to receive a call at 11 PM, this added an edge to their shock and apprehension.

Vern was first to respond. He removed the phone from its base and read the digital display. "It's my parents."

"Vern," began a shaky voice. "It's Dad. Your mother's in the hospital."

Vern sat abruptly on the bed and Marla sat next to him, waiting silently for the call to end. He said to his father, "I'll be there as soon as I can."

He recounted what his father had told him: that his mother had been experiencing severe abdominal pain for a while. Tonight it was the worst it had ever been. Coupled with her recent loss of weight, chronic diarrhea, and yellowing of the skin, her family doctor suspected pancreatic cancer.

"Shall I call for a substitute?" asked Marla. She was an art teacher at Indian River High School who rarely missed a day of work, so it was pretty certain that she could take off for such an emergency.

"No, I think I should check it out first. Then you can come down if need be."

Vern booked a flight for the next afternoon to Orlando.

2

*****

Vern's previous boss, Darryl, had moved to St. Croix four years earlier and opened up a computer repair shop in Gallows Bay. In turn, Vern opened a small shop in Bethany Beach where he met with immediate success diagnosing and repairing home computers. He had two technicians who could take charge, so in the morning he made some calls setting everything in order for an undetermined time period.

He remembered when Marla's mother had suffered from breast cancer and they had been able to keep her at their condo for the last few months of her life. He wished his own mother didn't live so far away, but the Alexanders had dreamed of retiring in Florida where they had lived the past fifteen years. They had been so intent in making the move that when they sold their home in Pennsylvania, it was left completely furnished except for a few pieces of furniture his mother couldn't bear to part with. Although he often seemed gruff on the exterior, Vern shared this sentimentality and kept his dark cherry bedroom set, which Marla always complained didn't go with their beach décor. She was right, of course, but that touch of nostalgia demanded that he keep some pieces of his past. He thought maybe someday he could let go of them, but he wasn't ready yet. Now with his mother's mortality being challenged, the bedroom set of his past became dearer to him, along with the refinished hutch his mother had distressed with his father's rasp and some old nails. She had antiqued it herself, a work of art that took up far too much space in their tiny dining area.

"Do you want me to take off work and drive you to the airport?" Marla asked as she put the clean coffee cups into the hutch.

"No. Save the days off in case you need them later." Vern reached for his iPhone. "Stay right there. Let me get your picture for my mother in front of her old hutch. She'll like that." Vern was always sending pictures to his parents with his phone. He'd made them both learn to skype and become techno-savvy even though many of his parents' friends didn't even own a computer.

*****

Pancreatic cancer, he thought to himself, as he drove up Coastal Highway to the Philadelphia International Airport. He had never heard of anyone surviving it. Maybe it was something else. His father had used the word *suspected*; the doctor *suspected* pancreatic cancer. He was surprised at the tears that sprang to his eyes at the thought he might lose his mother. They talked each week on the phone, and even though he saw his parents only once or twice a year, he felt close to them like they were right around the corner from him.

He supposed he was a "Mama's boy" in his formative years, sticking close to home, obeying her rules, not causing her to ever have to say, "Wait till your father gets home!" Vern idolized his mother and saw her as the mother every boy should have. He smiled as he remembered her warmth, how they used to snuggle in front of the fireplace while she read him stories like *Go Dog Go* and *Are You My Mother?*

He reflected how his choice of Marla as a wife was so influenced by his mother's personality. The two women shared the love of art. Both were sensitive and intuitive. They possessed a strength of character and some of the same physical characteristics. Marla's slender build, her hazel eyes with the green flecks, and her spontaneous smile were all similar to his mother's. His father had said to him on their second anniversary, "Vern, you married your mother," a compliment from the man who adored Katherine Alexander as much as did his son.

Traffic slowed as he neared the Dover Air Force Base. A C-141 passed overhead on a training flight. He watched as it dipped toward the landing strip and then lifted again as the pilot practiced his skills. Watching the progress in his rearview mirror, he beamed at the memory of when he had flown on a jumbo cargo plane from St. Croix and landed at the base. He thought about the Vern who was so careless about his relationship with his wife at that time, how he had doubted her intuition and dismissed her deepest feelings. He often paid more attention to his computer screen and video games than to her. She had tried to involve him in several issues in the past, but he was completely oblivious to her enthusiasm. Now he was a changed man, one who relied on Marla's companionship and support. He realized how lucky he was to have the strength of their love for each other.

His reflections drifted back to his mother. She had been the strong one who provided the compass for his father and him. She had guided him through some rough high school days when he was on the verge of hanging with the wrong crowd, had helped his father when he lost his job, had welcomed Marla into their lives and let him know she thought Marla was the *one*. Katherine Alexander was in her early 60s, too young to be taken from him, too young to leave his father a widower. Marla's mother had been young, too, when she lost her battle to cancer. Unlike his wife, Vern had no unsettled business with his mother, no longstanding resentments, feelings of being unloved, things unspoken over the years. Or so he thought.

The Essington exit was nearly upon him when Vern awoke from his thoughts. He had been driving on "automatic pilot" the past several minutes in spite of the traffic on I-95 but saw the turn-off in time to make the exit. He watched carefully until he saw the entrance off Industrial Highway to the remote parking lot and proceeded to the ticket booth. Looks more like an entrance to a park than a parking lot, he thought. Marla would appreciate the banks of petunias, shrubs, forsythia and recently appearing tulips. So would his mother. She loved this time of the year in the Northeast and had come north for a visit a few times just to see the floral displays at the Philadelphia Flower Show and Longwood Gardens.

He had never used the parking facility before but quickly adapted to the situation, pulled a ticket from the automated machine and proceeded to the agent's window.

"Good afternoon," he said to the attendant.

"Howdy," replied the man. He leaned forward, squinting below the visor of his blue cap. "Didya know your gas cap's hangin'open?" His beefy arm extended from the window as he pointed to the side of Vern's Honda SUV.

Vern craned his neck to look back at the hanging cap on the driver's side of the car. "Damn," he said, and got out of the car to reattach the cap. "Must be a sign of old age creeping up. I have a lot on my mind this morning and can't seem to get on track." He regretted that he hadn't allowed Marla to take the day off to drive him to the airport. It struck him that she watched over him as his mother had and he cursed himself for being so careless. He realized he had begun to be careless about a number of things, a disquieting thought to the Vern who Marla accused of being almost anal.

"I like to think that's not age-related," said the attendant. "I been absent-minded since I was about ten years old."

As he pulled away, he thought of the gas cap and perseverated on his growing forgetfulness - glossing over details, forgetting appointments, leaving the house without his office keys. He remembered how Marla used to do things he considered silly and irresponsible when she was overwhelmed; now he was doing the same. His mother used to tell him that memory was a matter of paying attention, and he rationalized that his failings were not a loss of memory, just that he was not giving full focus to tasks at hand. But he questioned whether this new habit creeping into his life signaled something more serious. Neither of his parents had exhibited any

7

signs of mental lapses. He had no other living relatives, so he wasn't sure if dementia or the dreaded Alzheimer's was part of his genetic entitlement.

Vern continued to be pre-occupied in his thoughts as he waited in the check-in line, took off his shoes through security, and settled into the departure lounge, coffee in hand and a new Harlan Coben novel at the ready. At the waiting area, he slouched in his chair, stretching his legs, wiggling his toes in his worn deck shoes, preparing for the flight. Vern's long frame always presented a problem when flying, a fact that sometimes prompted road trips by car or travel by train. Marla didn't like to fly from fear but his avoidance was strictly from discomfort. This was another trait Marla shared with his mother – the fear of flying. She had improved; in fact they had taken three vacations in the past four years - one to Europe, one to Hawaii, and to Florida. Vern had insisted on Amtrak to Florida last year due to the cramped position on airplanes, but in this case, saving time was important.

His thoughts returned to his mother's health. Vern's logical nature told him there was nothing he could do but wait until he got there, that worrying wouldn't make his mother better in the short or long run, so he opened his book and began to read. He read the first page three times, each time chastising himself for not focusing, especially after having had this conversation earlier with himself specifically about focusing. He wanted to be like his favorite Coben character, Myron Bolitar, and solve all of life's mysteries. He wanted to know all the details of his mother's illness. He wanted to know now. Vern had never been one for exhibiting endless patience, and the time and distance separating him from this dilemma were starting to throw him into an abyss.

Two rows behind him a baby wailed. Oh no, he thought, the kid will probably be sitting next to me on the plane. He picked up his carry-on and moved to a window facing the tarmac and sat in a rocking chair. Pushing himself back and forth, he blankly stared out as he watched planes taxi to the nearby gates. His aircraft was moored to the passenger walkway. He watched scurrying workers pump jet fuel, load baggage, stow food supplies, and check off lists on clipboards. He wondered why they were loading food but realized that it was just snacks and drinks for the domestic flight, a sign of the times. He knew Southwest had no first class seats, but one of Vern's dreams was that he could fly first class everywhere he went. He caught himself daydreaming of being pampered with mimosas as he boarded and immediately pinched his left earlobe, the sting of it bringing him back to the reality of his mother's condition and why he was on this flight. He was ashamed that he wasn't wishing only for her good health.

When a passenger service agent finally announced it was time to board, Vern went immediately to the gathering line and fretted his way onto the plane, watching to see where the crying baby would sit. He and Marla had made the decision not to have children, and he was in no mood to have to tolerate a fussy child next to him. There would be no relaxation for him until he could see his mother. He hoped it would not be for the last time.

9

*****

Vern laid his laptop on the front seat, then settled his suitcase into the trunk of the rental car. After programming the GPS for the hospital's address, he began his journey. It was north of his parents' home, so he needed to focus only on the traffic. All the familiar landmarks were a blur – the nuclear cooling towers, the prison, the numerous canals. The nine-foot alligator enjoying the afternoon sun alongside the highway diverted his attention from worrying about his mother. He'd have to tell Marla about that. He wondered if she would think these were ominous sights he was seeing on his way to his mother's bedside and he resumed worrying. He thought of the owl and its sudden appearance the night before. Ordinarily, Vern didn't give a lot of thought to such coincidences. Besides, hadn't one Nanticoke staff member said that some of the people of that tribe thought the owl brought good luck? But this was his mother he was going to see, who had banked on coincidences her entire life. She had always insisted everything happened for a purpose.

What a coincidence it was that Marla taught at Indian River High School in Delaware and his mother lay suffering in Indian River Memorial Hospital in Vero Beach. The two had so many connections to each other. Was it a coincidence he had met Marla, of all places, at his mother's birthday party? That summer at the beach when she was a waitress in Bethany Beach and he was a lifeguard, the two most important women in his life connected. She had been the waitress who so impressed his mother one day at lunch that she called the restaurant

10

and arranged for her to wait on their table for her birthday dinner. His mother was pleased when she saw how Vern watched her throughout the entire meal and afterward asked her for her phone number.

His cell phone rang. He noted the display as he brought the phone to his ear.

"Hi Dad," he said. "I'm about ten minutes from the hospital, according to TomTom. How's Mom doing?"

"She's awake for the time being, so this will be a good time for you to come. She had a rough night but has been resting off and on."

He could hear the fear in his father's voice. "And how are you holding up? You sound tired."

"I have to admit I didn't get much sleep last night. They let me stay outside intensive care. I could come in every hour for a few minutes. Of course, she was sedated and didn't know I was there."

Vern could imagine his father's furrowed brow, how his gray stubble would have grown out, how he would be rubbing at it nervously. He hated being unshaven, and he was sure, even during this crisis, his father would be irritated by the growth.

"Is she still in intensive care?" An edge developed in Vern's voice which he knew his father would detect.

"No," he said, a breath of relief evident. "She was moved into this room this morning." Vern's mind could see him waving his arm, pointing to his wife and the surroundings, as though Vern could see. Relieved, Vern sought to lighten his father's situation by joking. "How's that five o'clock shadow of yours doing?"

James Alexander answered, "You know how I love this look. When you get here, I'm going home to shave, shower, and change clothes."

Vern grinned as he imagined his father running his hand down his grizzled cheek and across his chin. Consulting TomTom, he said, "I need to hang up. Looks like I'm on top of you. What's the room number?"

*****

Vern's father looked up as the ambient sound of the hospital corridor entered when Vern opened the door. He rushed over to him and hugged him close. "I'm so glad you're here," he said, and motioned toward his wife, who had lapsed into sleep. "She's been dozing off and on, just nodded off again about two minutes ago."

"You look like you could nod off yourself. When you go home for the shower and shave, take a nap in your own bed. I'll stay here with Mom." He looked over at her sleeping form and inched closer, his father still holding onto him. "Don't worry. If we need you, I'll call you right away."

James Alexander stroked his wife's arm, leaned over and kissed her forehead, and clutched at his son's arm. "I was so afraid I was going to lose her last night." He looked over at her and Vern could tell as his father's chin trembled that he was thinking about the fact that he *was* going to lose her if the doctor's suspicion was correct. They had addressed this issue several times in the past year, but Katherine had dismissed her symptoms as indigestion or stress. Their family doctor had warned her that she should have some tests done. She always said that if you went to the doctor, he'd find something wrong even if you were healthy as a horse.

"Let's hope for the best, Dad. Go home and get some rest." He walked with his father to the door and hugged him again. "I'll watch over her until you get back." He watched his father shamble down the light green corridor, past the evening dinner carts and candy-stripers hurrying back and forth. Vern could tell by the workers' beaming faces that, despite his worries, James Alexander was forcing a smile as he nodded a greeting to them along the way. He thought about the good fortune he had enjoyed having two such caring parents.

He took up the vigil at his mother's bedside, watched the monitor above her measuring her heart rate and blood pressure. He surveyed the array of tubes coming from her and wondered what each one was. Looking at the chart at the foot of her bed, he knit his brow at the frowning emoticon face which indicated his mother's pain level. He would have to ask why the letters NPO were written on the chart. The methodical sound of the drip going into her veins took his attention and he followed the fluids from two separate dangling cords coursing down from bags hanging on an IV pole.

He studied his mother's face, traced the faint wrinkles on her forehead, down her cheeks, the laugh lines at her eyes. He noticed how age spots had popped up here and there and marred her milky skin, how her veins showed across her knuckles and wrists, how his mother had aged. Although she was no longer a young vibrant woman, he knew she loved him as much as she always had, unconditionally. He grimaced at the

13

invasion of the tubes, the tape anchoring them in place, the way they pulled at her skin. He noticed for the first time the line at her pale scalp, how gray roots were taking over.

Katherine Alexander opened her eyes and stared into Vern's face. He could see the recognition register as her eyes widened.

"You're one in a million," he whispered into her ear. Her familiar smile spread in its familiar way. He saw the lights go on in her eyes first, then the lips puckered and straightened before pulling back to reveal a toothless gap on the upper right side where her partial dentures should have been. She brought a shaky hand up to cover it, but he took her hand and said, "Go ahead – I want to see that look – teeth or no teeth."

Vern cradled her close, stroking her and humming 'One little, two little, three little Indians.' "Remember how you'd sing that to me at night?"

"First thing we did was the bedtime story," she said, her voice trembling, rising and falling with each difficult breath. "That was never enough. You'd never let me leave the room without singing that."

"I sing it now and then to our new kitten instead of 'Soft kitty, warm kitty,'" Vern told her and hummed the kitty song to his mother. This was something he'd never admit to his guy pals, but this tender and playful side gave him major points with Marla.

She closed her eyes and drifted back into a drugged sleep as he gently settled her onto her pillow. Tears spilled over onto his cheek and he hoped she wouldn't wake up and see them. He leaned back into the hard-backed chair and stretched his legs, pulled back his kneecaps and flexed his ankles. He walked over to the sink where he poured cold water from the tap, doused his head and neck, then went back to the chair next to his mother.

He thought how the past week he'd done no running, lifting, or other routines he usually performed to keep in shape. His fortieth birthday was approaching, but he had the body of a twenty-five year old, due to the regimen he practiced faithfully. If only he could transfer that vigorous health into his mother's faltering body.

Vern pulled his Coben book from his briefcase, opened it to the beginning again but had no better luck than he'd had at the airport or on the plane. His phone vibrated in his pocket. He stepped into the hallway just as a nurse was entering the room. "I'll call you back in a few minutes," he said to Marla, as he followed the nurse to his mother's side. "She's sleeping," he told her.

"I can see that," the nurse answered. She started her ministrations anyway, recording vital signs and placing the chart back in its place. She was gone within a minute, so fast that Vern forgot to ask her about the NPO designation. She had done her work so efficiently she didn't wake his mother.

"Do you want me to come down?" Marla asked when they resumed their conversation.

"I think we should wait to see what the diagnosis is and how long she'll need to stay in the hospital."

"Well, give her my love when she wakes up – Dad, too. I'm going to pack a bag so I'll be ready whenever you want me there "

Fran Hasson

Want her there, Vern thought. He wanted her there right now, but he had to get all the details first before putting her through all the trouble of coming down. It all depended on what the doctor had to say tomorrow. For now, Vern tried to be patient and wait at his mother's side, although he, along with everyone who knew him well, understood that patience was not his forte.

Chapter 2

I shall be as secret as the grave.
Miguel Cervantes *Don Quixote*

SHE DRIFTED in and out of consciousness. The pain had been unbearable. Now this fuzzy state she was in blocked out the pain, but her mind was in a cloud. Her thoughts faded and re-appeared. For a few minutes she even imagined Vern was there. Her baby. The image of his face was wavy. He was not a baby – he was a grown man. He was singing to her, the *Ten Little Indian* song. Blissful sleep took over again.

"Dad, when will the doctor be in to talk to us?"

She heard Vern's voice. Katherine Alexander struggled to sit up but her son came to her and put a gentle hand on her shoulder.

"Mom," he said, "be careful. You'll drag those tubes right out of your arms."

She looked up at the hoses supplying her and down at the one draining her, across at the wires monitoring her. Her expression changed with each shift of the eyes.

17

She went from frowning to knitting her eyebrows together, finally looking at Vern. She said, "They sure have me hog-tied don't they?"

Vern's grin spread the same as his mother's from the lighting of the eyes to the puckering of the lips, to the showing of a mouthful of his teeth. She responded with a mirror image beam. When can I tell him, she asked herself. Her smile faded and his concerned look alarmed her. Oh no, he'll think I'm in pain, she thought, and managed another cheerful expression.

"When did you get here?" she asked. "I've caused you so much trouble." She scanned the room. "Is Marla here?"

Vern propped her up on her pillow. "There," he said, "is that better? Does anything hurt?" When he was sure she was comfortable, he continued. "Marla's at home. I thought I'd come down first and see how you are and then she can join us. But she's here in spirit – see, she's already sent flowers." He pointed to the vase of gladiolas on the bedside table.

Katherine delighted at seeing the vase and considered Vern's remark. She figured he meant: *to see if you're going to make it.* She remembered the trip in the ambulance to the hospital. Some of the fuzziness was clearing, but at the same time, the pain was returning. Phrases and comments came back to her. Pancreatic cancer was the last term that she remembered before the sedatives took effect. Is that what's wrong with me, she thought.

"Do you know what's wrong with me?" she asked her son. "Do I have pancreatic cancer?"

She was a very intelligent woman who kept up with news on all fronts - politics, sports, medicine. She knew that type of cancer was almost certainly a death sentence and if that was what she had, she wanted to know. There were so many loose ends in her life, most of which were insignificant: her secret recipes which she would never divulge, the quilt she was working on, the stash of five-dollar bills she'd been hiding away for the past ten years, but the secret she'd been hiding from Vern all his life was with her every day. She *had* to tell him. Or she would die, leaving it to James to be the bearer of the news. Was it really necessary to tell him, anyway? What difference would it make to him? She would wait until she got the diagnosis.

"I was just talking with Dad on the phone. He'll be back here soon. Says the doctor will consult with him tomorrow."

"With *him*?" she said. "What about *me*? Don't I need to be in on this?"

"Talk to Dad about it."

She remembered Vern in his youth, not wanting to get in the middle of a parental disagreement. Not that they disagreed often in front of their son, but she thought of the times when Vern played one against the other the way kids will do and if he got away with something and the other found out about it, he'd say, "Talk to Dad about it," or "Talk to Mom about it." She smiled in spite of the situation. "You bet I will," she said.

He beamed, and Katherine wondered if he was remembering the same scenarios and her same response from years ago.

James Alexander arrived, rested, shaven, and in fresh clothes. He leaned over to kiss his wife and announced they'd have to leave soon, that visiting hours were nearly over. Vern went out into the hall to use the visitors' restroom and Katherine said to her husband, "I need to tell him, James." She grimaced in pain, both from the disease's physical toll and the emotional burden she bore.

"Give it some time. Rest and when you feel better, we'll discuss it."

"Give it some time? Hasn't thirty-seven years been enough time?" Her eyes begged him. "Do I have cancer? Is the doctor going to tell me? I want to know. I can't go to my grave without telling Vern." She looked nervously around the room, her eyes darting from the door to her husband as though Vern could have slipped through unseen and was standing right there.

"There, there, my sweet Katherine," James whispered to her. "Everything will be all right. Vern will understand. Or if you don't tell him, that'll be OK, too."

Vern re-appeared and caught the end of his father's consoling words.

She flinched at the sight of her son. She knew he'd been there for the last sentence and hoped he thought it meant her diagnosis, that he would understand if she didn't tell him that.

Vern looked at his mother, then his father, the question burning in his eyes. Katherine tried to inch her way higher on her pillow but the effort was painful, and James tried to help her into position. The question went unanswered as the two men comforted their beloved patient. Katherine closed her eyes and secretly applauded her Sarah Bernhardt move, tightened her jaw as she knew she had erased the provocative sentence from their immediate thoughts.

"That's better," she said. She implored her husband, "Don't you think they'll let you stay just a little longer. Vern just arrived here. Surely they'll give us a few more minutes."

The loudspeaker sounded in the hallway and echoed in the wall-mounted speaker over the door, a somewhat seductive voice trying to blunt the message: "Visiting hours will soon be over. You may return tomorrow from 11 AM to 8:30 PM. Thank you for your observance."

They all exchanged glances and although she would have liked them to remain longer, Katherine was pleased they would have to leave before the question would return that had burned in Vern's eyes.

Before her two men left for the evening, Katherine received another round of medication. She drifted into a twilight setting, fought it, opened her eyes and forced them to stay wide. I have to find the right words, she thought, the right way to tell him. Will he hate me for what's left of the rest of my life? Will he hate me into eternity? Was I wrong to keep this secret? Was I wrong to force James to keep it with me?

She couldn't will her eyes to stay open any longer and soon fell into a troubled sleep, tossing and turning through the night. A nurse came in to check vitals and reported on her chart that she kept saying. "I'm sorry… Forgive me," in her drugged unconsciousness.

Throughout the night, Katherine woke and sank back into a troubled sleep. Flashbacks of a three-year old Vern, chubby and blonde, carrying his favorite stuffed shark everywhere, brought smiles to her fretting face. She picked him up and whirled him around in her semi-conscious state. "Forgive me," she cried out, and lapsed into sleep again and again. Sometimes she was whirling him around, sometimes playing hide and seek in the staircase that wound from the kitchen to the second floor, around through his bedroom and down the center staircase into the main hallway. Sometimes he was racing across the lawn and hiding under the enormous blue Atlas cedar tree, clutching his shark and she'd find him, pull him out playfully, and clutch him with all her might to her chest and sob, "Forgive me!"

On one such occasion, a nurse rushed in and moved quickly to her bedside. "Mrs. Alexander, are you okay?" She checked the assortment of tubes and wires. "Your monitor was beeping." It was the same nurse who had given her the sedative earlier. She was strong and adept at managing patients and settled Katherine into a comfortable position. "I keep hearing you call out, 'Forgive me.' I can't imagine you have anything that needs forgiving." She stroked her hair and ran her fingers down Katherine's cheek and looked at her patient so sadly that Katherine felt she would cry.

Katherine was so moved by the nurse's compassion that she decided to share some of her predicament with her, the sharing of difficult matters sometimes easier with strangers. "I don't know if I'm going to die, and I have something on my conscience I need to confess," she explained. "When I do, I'm afraid my son will hate

22

me for all eternity." She pulled at her blanket and avoided the nurse's eyes, first glancing at the bedside table where Marla's bouquet sat, then at the ceiling where one long fluorescent bulb in the housing fluttered sporadically, back to the IV tubes and then squarely at the nurse.

"Ma'am, I've been in this business for thirteen years now and I can guarantee that your son can handle anything you can tell him. I can tell what kind of woman you are – you can't hide goodness and love, even under all those tubes and wires." She lightly touched Katherine's face again. "Now you just think good thoughts and consider what kind of life you've led. Trust your son."

What kind of a life have I led? thought Katherine, after the nurse left. She knew her life was not one of turmoil, that she had raised her son in a peaceful environment and had been there for him until the day he left home. That she had loved his wife and accepted her into the family as the daughter they never had. Vern had been the center of Katherine and James's world. They had protected, nurtured, and given him all the love they had. Perhaps the nurse was right; perhaps she should just trust him to put it in the proper perspective and go on.

*****

Katherine opened her eyes and yawned, forgetting the IV tubes as she tried to cover her mouth. "Damn ropes," she muttered and reached toward the night table, grabbing at her crown and bridge but unable to grasp the denture. She manipulated the alarm cord and called for a nurse. The sun had risen and she glimpsed the tops of palm trees and scattered beeches, her first chance to see outside her room since she'd been admitted.

"Mrs. Alexander, you're bright-eyed and bushy-tailed this morning," sang an employee as she pushed a cart into the room.

"I'm usually up before the sun. You've got me so doped up here I missed the sunrise," she complained. "Do you have any food on that contraption for me?"

The woman told her she still wasn't allowed anything until the doctor gave the go-ahead. "I'm here to take from you instead of giving," she explained. "I'm what you call a phlebotomist although some call us vampires," she joked. She proceeded to draw several vials of blood, capped them, and jotted something on her record.

Katherine looked at the clock. "It's seven o'clock in the morning. Can't I at least get a cup of coffee?"

The phlebotomist apologized as she directed her cart from the room. "Sorry, ma'am, but your instructions say nothing by mouth until further notice – NPO."

When the woman disappeared, Katherine remembered her partial plate. Oh well, she thought, no need to put 'em in – nothing to eat, no one else to talk to. She settled back onto her pillow and replayed scenes from Vern's youth. She recalled how needy he was when he was young. How he clung to her and cried when she'd leave the room. She had adopted a dog when she and James moved to Florida. The dog had separation anxiety, probably from having been abandoned as a puppy, and it had taken them years to convince their pet that they weren't going to leave him.

So it was with Vern. She remembered a stretch of time from his third birthday lasting nearly a year until one day, shortly before he turned four. That was when he took the babysitter's hand and led her to the playroom after kissing his mother and father good-night. He didn't even look back at them as they stood in the doorway, waiting to do the usual consoling and promising to be "right back." That was the moment they realized he felt safe, secure with them.

She looked at the clock again. It seemed to stand still, the hands locked in place, visiting hours an eternity away. Would she be able to tell Vern today? When would the doctor be there? How long did she have? Was she going to die? Questions flooded in one after the other, paralyzing her. I'm just going to have to "woman up," she thought. This is so crazy. I'm driving myself stark-raving mad.

An attendant came in, propelling a gurney toward her as though he were driving in a Motocross event. She pulled her sheet up under her chin. He saw her startled look and apologized, but the smirk that flickered on his face irritated her. "I'm sorry, ma'am. This is my first day here and I don't have the hang of this durn wheelie yet."

Her irritation vanished as she recognized his hangdog look and remembered Vern when he'd brought the frog in from the pool surface skimmer, the way he laughed at her fright but knew he was in trouble and had to show remorse. She knew this young man was having the time of his life with the gurney, probably an after-, or in this case, before-school job. "Well, are you going to take me for a ride on that? Is that why you're in here?"

"Yes, ma'am. I have to take you down for an MRI."

"How're you going to get me off this bed with all these gadgets hooked up to me?"

A nurse entered the room and the question was answered when she effortlessly moved her with all the accompanying tubes and paraphernalia. She accompanied them on the journey to assure that everything moved smoothly. Katherine wished her husband and son were with her, that she could talk to the doctor and hear what had to be said. She felt better this morning, the acute and disabling pain gone, the nausea that wracked her before she came to the hospital replaced by hunger. She felt hopeful that it was a gallbladder attack, but the words *pancreatic cancer* kept coming back, those words that she had heard when she was supposedly unconscious but cognizant of what was being spoken.

*****

Vern and James came into her room promptly at 11:00. She watched the pair approach her bed. They were so different in appearance – Vern tall and slender with thick dirty blonde hair and cobalt blue eyes and James average in height, his once brown hair now thin and gray, the receding hairline revealing a broad forehead peppered with age spots. Cataracts dimmed his hazel brown eyes, but his mind, like his son's, was alert and receptive to all that went on around him.

James helped his wife put her partial plate in. The duty nurse had told him she could have it in place but she needed to remove it before he left for the day as she would be sedated for the evening. She also told him the doctor would make his rounds that afternoon.

The two men sat on each side of the bed. When the doctor came in carrying a clipboard and wearing a solemn expression, they stood to greet him. Katherine straightened herself, smoothed the sheet and ran her fingers through her hair. She wondered why she felt she needed to spruce up for someone who was probably going to deliver a death sentence. She wondered if the MRI results were in, if the numerous vials of blood had been processed, if he would tell her or if he would only tell her husband.

"Good afternoon. I'm Howard Montreau, your internist," he said to Katherine.

My internist, she thought, *my* internist. Looks like he'll give *me* the news.

He nodded toward the men and shook hands with James, who was on his side of the bed. Pulling the curtain around the bed to shield them from onlookers, he said, "Would you please step outside while I examine Mrs. Alexander?" directing his gaze toward the two.

Katherine didn't want to hear the news alone. "James, stay here," she said and sent a distinct eye signal to the doctor that she would not be challenged. Apologetically, she turned to Vern, but he was already moving away from the bed.

"It's okay, Mom," he said. "I understand. I'll go downstairs and have coffee and try to reach Marla."

After Vern left the room and the doctor had finished his examination, he stowed his stethoscope into his breast pocket and finished jotting notes on her chart. He pulled up a chair next to James. As he shuffled through some papers, he said, "The results have come back with all indications that you do, in fact, have a growth on your pancreas, which the ER doctors had suspected. There is a chance that the mass is benign, but we must take every step to investigate further."

Katherine's face fell and James moved closer and held her hand. "What happens next?" she said, with a brave clenching of the jaw and determined pursing of the lips.

"The good news is that the mass is at the head of the pancreas and is relatively small. We need to have a cardio work-up to see if you can withstand surgery, but I must caution you that with your recent weight loss, our first surgery will be to insert some stents to allow your digestive juices to flow and put some weight back on. Then when you're stronger, we can remove the tumor."

"Am I going to die?" Katherine looked at the doctor and then James. She saw tears forming in James's eyes and squeezed his hand, returning the comforting touch he had been giving her.

"I'm hoping we've caught it in its early stages. Your lymph nodes are not swollen. If it is indeed malignant, the good news is that it may be stage 1 or stage 2. We won't know exactly until we open you up."

Katherine thought back to the times the family doctor had advised her to have tests done. Surely James had told the surgeon how this condition had probably been developing for more than a year.

His tone was pedantic, like a dull professor delivering a lecture. Katherine had expected him to sound like a judge handing down a death sentence during the penalty phase of a trial. Somehow his medical bearing calmed Katherine, held off her impulse to break down, and gave her the courage to face whatever was in store for her.

"Can't you do a biopsy now," James asked, "so we know whether or not it's cancerous?"

"At this point," explained the doctor, "it doesn't make a difference. It must be removed. During the surgery, we biopsy it, and depending on how invasive it is, the surgery proceeds from there."

"Meaning?" Katherine dreaded his answer but knew in advance what he'd say.

"Meaning we'll know if the surgery will be advantageous to you."

His penetrating look cut into her like a scalpel. All she could do was nod and grip James harder.

*****

As they waited for Vern to return, Katherine scanned the walls, looking for courage, for a needlepoint sampler that said "When the going gets tough, the tough get going," or "When you can't change the direction of the wind, change your sails," or any of the pieces she had produced that were hanging in their home. The pale green walls stared back at her, offering no such succor. She looked from the wall-mounted TV, to the hand sanitizer fixture, to the loudspeaker, IV pole, and shiny metal nightstand to the hospital-issue atomic white-faced clock. Marla's beautiful bouquet of gladiolas resting on the bedside table next to her provided the only beauty in the room.

"I'm telling him today, James." She took a deep breath and let it out slowly. "When he comes back, we'll tell him what the doctor said, and then I want you to disappear for a while."

"Katherine, I'm staying here. I'm as much to blame as you are for keeping this secret so long. I want to help him process it, too." James's face was set. He didn't often challenge Katherine, in fact deferred to her in almost all important matters in their marriage.

But she recognized his conviction and acquiesced. In fact, she was a little relieved to think of him sharing this moment with her, supporting her, helping to explain it, helping to answer Vern's expected questions.

When Vern returned, he smiled, as though to bolster his courage, and asked, "Did they lift the NPO yet?" The atmosphere in the room was tense and Katherine saw the wheels in his head turning the way they did as a youth. She thought back to the time he came home and knew the report cards had been mailed out. She had seen him rifling through the mail on the table and wondered what he'd do if he spotted the familiar Wallingford School District logo. Would he slip it into his backpack? She had felt the tension in the air when he saw her looking from the hallway of their home. She knew he was assessing the attitudes of his parents now, as an adult, the same way he did as a teenager and sensed that it was not a good time for joking.

Chapter 3

High instincts which before our mortal nature
Did tremble like a guilty thing surprised
Truths that wake,
To perish never.
William Wordsworth
Ode to Intimations of Immortality

VERN SAT NEXT TO his mother, on the side of the bed across from his father. His leg bumped against the metal nightstand, jarring the vase of flowers. Quickly he righted the container before the flowers could tumble out. "Caught 'em," he joked, but noticed his parents were looking subdued. Katherine's attitude seemed to have changed from the perky look she'd had before the examination. She was crestfallen, gray with the yellow tint returning that his father had talked about. He knew the news was not good and reached over to take her hand to try to ease the telling of it.

The distended veins on her wrists and hands were more prominent, as though the blood was gushing through them in her nervous excitement. The tape which

31

held the IV tubes in place were dams, staying the onrushing flow through the vessels.

He remembered her strong arms when he was a young child as she hoisted him over her head. One night on her way out to a masquerade party, she pushed her pouty bright red lips at him. "Kiss the Lipstick Queen good-night," she said and planted a Tammy Faye Bakker tattoo on his cheek, pinning him against her Betty Boop dress; then she waved good-bye as she and his father raced off. He wanted to kiss her now, as he remembered that scary jet black wig she wore and the bright red lips but held back, the sad look on her face so different from the cheerful one years ago. Now the strong arms that had effortlessly held him tight were as motionless as the rest of her tired body.

He leaned closer as she began a labored conversation, breathing deeply between words. He figured the doctor's visit had leveled her; that was why she was far worse than she had been when he left the room. He was surprised when, instead of revealing what the doctor had told her, she looked at him with tears starting to flow. She said, "You were filled with such promise. There was never the right time to tell you."

Vern backed off a little and looked over to his father, whose eyes were downcast. "What..." he stammered, but she waved her free hand at him. He felt confused. *The right time?*

"I've wanted to tell you for years, but I waited too long and then it was easier not to tell you..." She paused, took a deep breath, and blurted out, "That you were adopted."

Vern released his grip on her hand and sat upright, stared unbelievingly, first at his mother, then his father. He could tell from her pained expression that now she was in more distress and knew he had to say something, but words were hard to form. This was a new mother lying there, contrite, confessing a secret she had harbored for years. A ghostly glow surrounded her and he was afraid she would draw her last breath if he responded incorrectly. But how should he respond?

He was a fake portrait of perfect composure. Later he would tell Marla about his command performance because at that very moment he was a tree stripped bare of its leaves from hurricane force winds, a skeleton shredded of any muscles or nerves, a child lost in a mall. His entire framework had been shattered. He found himself wondering who he really was.

"I'm so sorry," she said, "that I didn't tell you years ago. But if I don't beat this cancer thing, I can't go to my grave leaving it for your dad to tell you."

In the deepest place in his heart, Vern knew that her silence over the years had been to protect him, to shield him from harm. He knew if he displayed any anger, she'd detect it, and in her fragile state, he wanted to safeguard her. This suddenly vanished part of his past didn't shape his character or influence his present. He was who he was; whether it was because of nature or nurture made no difference. He knew he had to give her back the love she'd showered on him for all his life – his life that he could remember.

He took her hand again in both his hands, massaging them as he leaned forward, and kissed her forehead. "Did you think I wouldn't love you if you told me?" he asked. He glanced at his father, who flashed a look of recognition and approval between them.

She rolled her eyes up to him, a peaceful look spreading across her face in response. "Thank you for that," she said quietly. Her hand trembled in his grasp as she sought to return his tight grip and pull him closer.

Vern kissed her forehead again. "That must have been so hard for you to say after all these years."

When his mother's eyes closed and she seemed to be slipping into sleep, he rose slowly, releasing his hold on her and motioned his father to join him in the hallway.

The two men faced each other. Vern leaned against the wall after looking back into the room to see that his mother had drifted off. He folded his arms, shook his head, and looked at his father, the question burning in his eyes.

Sheepishly, James said, "I'm sorry, Vern. We just didn't know how to tell you. There were a few times we were determined to sit down and just lay it out there, but your mother...er, my wife..."

"Hold it, Dad. She's my mother and you're my father. Period." Trays carrying dinner were being pushed down the corridor. The aroma of cooked food filled the air, plates and cutlery clinked a background sound, and Vern directed his father to a small waiting room at the end of the corridor. "Let's sit in here a while before we go back in the room."

They sat facing each other, a chrome and glass table between them. Vern leaned forward in the cheap vinyl chair as did his father. "When, where, who? This is all so overwhelming," he said to his father.

A couple came into the room, accompanied by an elderly patient who was negotiating with a walker. "She wants to eat her dinner in here tonight. Do you mind?" the woman asked.

Vern thought, Yeah, really I do, but go ahead. He smiled at the couple and stood to take the tray from what he supposed was the daughter. "Here, let me put it here." He directed his comment at the elderly woman, who was concentrating on the placement of her walker while her son-in-law held her arm protectively. "It's good you're able to walk here to the dining room." He thought of his sleeping mother who still was unable to eat anything, how she would have been proud that he didn't point out the woman's mistake of thinking this location was an eating area. He and James went back into the hall while the three newcomers sat around the area they had been using as a conference table.

"We can talk about this at home," James said. "This will be an all-nighter, so we may as well be comfortable and private."

*****

"Guess what I found out today," Vern said to Marla as he drove back to his parents' home.

"That alligators don't live in Florida, that they're really crocodiles; that the moon is really made of cheese, that you miss me so much you want me on the next plane to Orlando," rattled Marla.

35

Taking the bait, Vern replied, "Alligators and crocodiles both live in Florida and I do want you right here right now, but this is a little more serious."

Marla remained quiet. In their years together, they could pick out from voice tones and facial expressions when the joking was inappropriate and this was one of those times, even unseen and at the faraway location.

"I'm not really Vern Alexander," he said. "In fact I don't have a clue as to who I am."

"What?"

"I just found out I was adopted. Mom is afraid she's going to die. It's pretty certain that she has pancreatic cancer."

"Oh, no," said Marla.

"She couldn't face surgery or treatment without telling me, so I guess you'd have to say I feel pretty perplexed right now. It's a double whammy – her so sick and now finding this out...." He told her that he and his father were going to have a long talk at home and he'd have more details later.

"Shall I come down now? My bags are packed. I have lesson plans for a week that I just need to run over to Sybil."

Vern pulled into his parents' driveway and sat back, leaning against the headrest. He blew a slow breath. "Come as soon as you can. Here comes the pizza delivery car. Gotta go now. I'll call you later before I turn in and fill you in on more. Dad's already at the door. I love you," he said.

"I'll be awake. Give Dad a hug for me."

Father and son sat at the dining room table as though it were a normal pizza night, eating slices of the pie and drinking Corona beer. Vern looked around at the samplers his mother had embroidered: *Home is where Vern is* caught his eye first. "I was the apple of her eye, wasn't I?"

"And mine, too," added his father.

"Of course. I'm sorry." Vern saw the pinched expression on his father's face, the furrowing of his brows, the quivering of his lips and knew that even though he was not as expressive as Katherine, James loved him as much as any natural father, probably even more.

His eyes teared as thoughts of his childhood rushed through. The notes his mother would put in his lunchbox – Q: What is a mathematician's favorite food? A: Apple pi; Q: What did pilgrims use to bake cake A: May-flour; the birthday cakes made into shapes of Snoopy, or jack-o-lanterns or whatever he wanted her to make; the never-ending love no matter what he did through all his life.

"So what can you tell me? When did you adopt me? I can't remember anything but you and Mom." But he knew that in growing up, he'd had what he called daydreams where other people were around him. Where small children played with him, where unknown adults would pick him up and swing him around, where strange names would resonate – Pru came to mind. These images would pop up on playgrounds, at movie theaters, during television shows, much like déjà vu.

"We adopted you right before your third birthday," his father said. "We had been hearing about you from a social worker your mother knew – Katherine, that is."

Vern could see that his father was uneasy now about his parents' place as his real parents, so he interrupted the conversation. "Dad, I told you before - you and Mom are my parents. You always will be, so don't qualify it by adding on any tags. If you want to differentiate when you're speaking about *them*, just call the other two my biological mother and father." Reaching for his beer, he proposed a toast. "Here's to the two people who loved me more than any two biological parents could ever love a child."

His father clicked his bottle against Vern's, adding, "And still do."

"Okay, who was the social worker, how did she know of me, where did I live, and how much energy do you have in your tank to go over this whole thing?" He found himself rubbing the back of his neck and twisting his left earlobe in the nervous way he often did.

"Vern, I have to admit I'm pretty exhausted from the stress of your mom. And I'm not trying to hide anything, but I'll try to give you enough to ponder for now. We can sift through all of this for as long as you want." His face darkened as he began the task of pouring the details into his son's bewildered soul. His son who had never doubted his existence, whose life had been an open book, his son whose life he and Katherine had orbited around. He had been their son and their sun. Now a cloud passed over them both, but he set out to tell the story.

"We were living in Maryland at the time and your mother worked in Human Services for Baltimore County. She and this friend of hers were at lunch one day when you came into the restaurant with your aunt and two cousins. Jenny, your mom's friend, pointed you out. You know how your mom won't go into pet stores because she can't bear to see the sight of the puppies and kittens in cages, hoping to be adopted. Well, you turned and looked at her as you climbed into the booth and in that moment, she fell in love with you. She said it was like you were saying, 'Could you love me? Won't you take me home?'" James smiled as he recalled the day Katherine came home and pleaded to adopt Vern. "We had been trying to have a child and her maternal instinct took over. I didn't stand a chance." He looked up guiltily and his eyes pleaded forgiveness. "Not that I didn't want you…"

"Dad, I understand. If Marla came home with an outrageous idea, I'd balk, too." He swigged his beer and rose to get another. "Another for you, too? I think this calls for a few beers tonight." Walking to the fridge, he turned and said, "Please don't apologize for anything. Like your old detective pal, Joe Friday, I just want to get the facts. Can you imagine what a shock this is to me? I'm almost forty years old and am just now finding that I'm not who I always thought I was."

He could see the anguish register again on his father's face. He knew how guilty he must have felt at concealing this secret for so many years, but he wanted his father to be able to tell all that he knew and wanted that to be as painless as possible, for both of them.

"Oh, but you are still who you've always been, my son," continued James. "From the beginning, you were a delight, full of energy, anxious to investigate everything, and so loving to your mother. Sometimes you were quite pre-occupied, immersed in whatever you were doing, oblivious to the world around you."

Vern could see the wheels turning in his father's head and imagined the vignettes that were playing through. Was he remembering the time he made his own Halloween costume, forbidding them from helping, telling him how "the teacher said we have to do it ourselves" and how even though other kids came in with papier-mâché creations, bright with enamel paint and articulated parts, how proud they were that he had won the prize. His robot, made from an old carton spray-painted silver and detailed with black magic marker, had been his own creation from the inception to the production. They were proud, not of the award, but of his determination and sense of fair play. Or when he joined the drama club and memorized massive amounts of dialogue, practicing before the mirror, reciting as he went through the house, stopping to orate to Christy, their beloved rescue mutt. Vern wondered again, had *he* been rescued? What kind of a life had he been leading? Why did he have a puppy dog look that day in the restaurant? What did his mother see in his eyes that made her so adamant about adopting him?

"Why was I with my aunt that day and not my mother? Was she alive? *Is* she alive? Do you know who she is?" Vern had so many questions. He realized that his staccato questions were as shocking to his father as the new knowledge was to him. He noticed his father's reaction to each rapid-fire question was a blinking of the eyes and a recoiling as though he were being attacked. He softened, lowering his voice. "Dad, I'm so sorry. Maybe I should just let you get some rest while I make a list of questions for you. Then we can go over them bit by bit, not all at once like this." Over the years, Vern was more comfortable at his computer than face to face with most people, so he relished the thought of composing himself, putting this into perspective, the tactile feeling of the keyboard a relaxant to him.

He saw his father relax for the first time since they'd left the hospital. "Yes, son, I think that's a good idea. There's so much to tell. It's probably best to tell you what you need to know first. All the details might just lead to more confusion."

Fran Hasson

Chapter 4

*The little world of childhood with its familiar surroundings is a
model of the greater world. The more intensively the family has
stamped its character upon the child, the more it will tend to feel and
see its earlier miniature world again in the bigger world of adult life.
Naturally this is not a conscious, intellectual process.*
Carl Gustav Jung

SHE HUGGED HER KITTEN close to her. "Sorry,
Marmalade," Marla said. "I'm going to have to leave
you for a few days." She remembered when she and
Vern had gone to St. Croix a few years back, leaving her
previous cat, Mo, for the first time ever. She laughed at
how he had snubbed them when they got back from the
trip. And how he knew after that whenever they were
going away, pouting and turning away from them on
their return. On one occasion Mo had stowed away in
their luggage. Marla had found him deep beneath the
clothing as she finished sorting things out and lifted him,
wiggling, from the suitcase.

The new kitten squeaked as he burrowed into her
chest, nestling like a baby wanting a bottle, staring into

43

her eyes and reaching one paw to her face. "I wish I could take you with me. Katherine would love you." She caressed his three buff and beige stripes running down his back.

Marla and Katherine Alexander were diehard animal lovers. It was Marla's dream to buy a house in the country where she could take in every stray cat that was abandoned or unloved. She knew Vern would never approve, even though he was a dog lover and would like to have had a yard for a dog to run in, so she did the next best thing and contributed to CATS (Cats Around Town Society) in Bethany Beach. She bought extra bags of cat food and donated funds to them.

She made her airline arrangements on the same flight Vern had taken. Next she arranged to have her friend and colleague, Sybil come each day to feed and play with her kitten. After that, she made the call to school for a substitute, having left plans with Sybil. As she was ready to settle in for the night, the phone rang. "Vern," she said, as she picked up the call. "How's everything going?"

"I'm making up a list right now of questions for my dad." Together they mulled over the matter. Questions poured out nonstop. "I can't type that fast," he said. "I don't know how much to push my dad right now with Mom the way she is. He looks almost as bad as she does."

Marla thought about the problem, not just as it concerned Vern, but how bereft his parents must be feeling, how they had kept that secret for so long, how they must have wanted to come clean, and how at this terrible juncture in their lives, they had to explain everything to him. She thought of her own mother in her final days, wasting away with cancer. So much had been left unsaid because her mother had never been one to take Marla into her confidence. She wondered if Theresa Collins had gone to the grave with deep, dark secrets, tortured through her last days with the inability to open up. It was only in her last week of life that she had looked up at Marla and whispered, "I love you." Tears sprang to her eyes at that memory. She recalled Vern saying to his parents at the end of every phone conversation, "I love you." This was not a phrase she had heard growing up.

"Okay, so what are the most important things you want to know right away, the ones that can't wait, that you might need to also ask of your mother while. . . " She broke off, thinking of how the ending of that sentence would seem too insensitive.

She knew Vern would end the sentence in his mind. They had the ability to read each other's thoughts, ending sentences for each other regularly. "One thing I want to know is about the birth certificate," he said. "Can you get it out of the safe deposit box before you fly? And bring it with you? I wonder why I was listed as Vern Alexander. I want to see the names listed as my parents. I'm pretty sure it had their names on it. Is that a fake? So I guess that's a good question to start with. Maybe they have a copy of my original birth certificate."

Marla's mind raced through their years together. She had thought a few times about the dissimilarity between him and his parents, his Nordic chiseled look, his height as he towered over the two of them, his bright blue eyes and theirs so different. Katherine's hazel eyes with the green flecks were more like Marla's, and James's hazel brown eyes held no resemblance to Vern's. Marla looked more like their daughter than he did their son. She remembered when James was diagnosed with diabetes and Vern went immediately for glucose testing but was assured by his parents it wouldn't happen to him. She had thought that a little curious at the time but figured, as usual, they were trying to support and protect him. Now she realized they might have been on the verge of telling him then about his parentage but couldn't follow through.

She thought of their wedding day and how sad it was that there were no cousins, aunts, uncles on Vern's side at their gala affair. He was an only child of two parents who had no siblings. Consequently no stories were passed down of his growing years, only the tales recounted by his parents, the numerous photo albums filled with memories of the three of them.

At least he had wonderful childhood memories, so different from her difficult life in a conflicted home with a mother who was dubbed the Iron Lady by her drunken and abusive husband. Her two brothers followed the trail their father had blazed for them and had tormented her for many of her formative years.

She had immediately fallen in love with Vern's parents. She often joked she married him so she could have them as parents. Her heart strained at the thought of Katherine dying and at the thought of the pain his parents were inflicting on themselves as they divulged this long-held secret. Part of her wished they had never told Vern. Another part knew he wouldn't let it go until he found out who his biological parents were. She knew he would pursue this mission with the same energy and vigor he exhibited at work, in the gym, playing games such as Team Trivia at the Fat Tuna Restaurant in Bethany Beach and Bonkers, and in everything he took on. But the greater part of her knew she would ultimately support him in his quest.

Suppose he couldn't locate his biological parents? Marla was full of apprehension about any search Vern might make for them. Suppose they were deceased? What if they were criminals? Did they really want to open this Pandora's Box?

"Vern, do you think your mother can handle the stress of your questioning? I think you have a good point about not pushing your dad too much right now. Do you think you should wait a while and just quietly research some of this?" Marmalade squeaked in the hallway, wagging his tail for a playtime session. Marla smiled in spite of the tense conversation and threw a toy mouse at the kitten. She wondered if bringing the kitten to Florida would cheer her mother-in-law up. His playfulness could provide therapy to her in this stressful time. Maybe she would assess the situation when she got down there and bring the little cat down for the next trip.

"Actually I think Mom will feel better talking about it, and Dad, too. And I want to find out as much as I can while my mother...." He broke off at the same thought as Marla had done. "I really believe it will make her feel better, no matter what happens with her condition. Can you imagine what a strain this has been?"

He looked around his bedroom. Although he had never lived there with his parents, the room resounded of Vern. A wall of certificates: lifesaving, debate awards, his high school and college diplomas, among others; trophies from peewee baseball up to Babe Ruth League; MVP awards; high school sports letters; childhood, graduation, and wedding pictures. It was practically a shrine to Vern. "I have to let her know without question that she and Dad are my true parents." He paused, his eyes sweeping over the Vern mementoes. "Knowing my parents, if I don't ask lots of questions, that will be worse. They'll think I'm mad at them for not telling me. I want to know and I have to know. We have to talk this out so my mother can recuperate or ... well, you know... go out in peace."

Marla wished she could be there at that moment, to hold Vern, to comfort him. He always showed a "stiff upper lip," a practice his father had carried with him from his British ancestors. She thought he'd inherited this trait but knew now he had learned it. She knew how he was hurting inside, though, and how having her there would help him face this challenge.

"You'll do the right thing, I'm sure," Marla said. "My flight gets into Orlando at 4:20. Think you can be there at that time to pick me up?"

"No problem. If anything comes up, I'll call you, but short of an extreme emergency with Mom, I'll be there waiting for you." He finished the Corona he'd carried into the room with him. "I think I'll try to sleep now. Well, maybe after I jot down a few more questions. Goodnight. I love you."

Marla kissed the mouthpiece of the phone and repeated the phrase to him. She thought to herself, I'm so glad I'll be able to help him. "Thank you, God," she whispered after hanging up. Marmalade leapt onto the bed and pounced at her. "Thank you, God, for this kitty, too."

*****

Vern and his father ate breakfast in the hospital cafeteria. His father was happy to not have any questions to answer that morning although he knew Vern was champing at the bit for information. Before leaving the house, Vern had told him he would ask nothing else until the stents had been put in and Katherine was out of the woods from that surgery.

The wheels of progress were turning fast. Katherine was scheduled to have the stents implanted the following morning. "Well, looks like they're already trying to fatten you up," Vern said as he and his father entered the room. Katherine was eating the last bite of toast on her tray.

"Funny how good dry toast tastes when you haven't eaten for days!" Katherine said. "Knowing this is the last sustenance I'll have for a while makes it very gourmet."

Even though Vern had promised not to ask questions, Katherine was anxious to talk about the adoption. She patted the bed, motioning for Vern to sit on the edge. "Remember when you'd come home from school and if you'd caught me napping, you'd climb up on the bed and stare at me on your hands and knees to be sure I was asleep?"

49

He laughed at the memory. "Yeah, I was always thinking about what I could get into but wanted to make sure you were down for the count. Especially around Christmas."

"For sure I had to be an expert hider of presents." She paused and took on a more somber expression. "Just as I hid your true identity."

He reached for her hand. "You really don't need to get into this right now. Let's wait till after your surgery, then we can discuss this."

"No," she said. "I want to talk about it now. Now that the floodgates are open, I want to let you know whatever you need to know."

She spent the next fifteen minutes getting the story off her chest, repeating some of what his father had told him. Vern could see the guilt leaving her, revealing the mother he'd known all his life. Color had returned to her face; wrinkles seemed to straighten. Her spirits were obviously lifted. She told him how she'd fallen in love with him at the restaurant, how that look he'd sent her was a signal that bound her to him. She'd gotten her friend, the social worker, to investigate the case and applied for the adoption papers.

"Apparently your birth mother had been shuttling you back and forth between your grandparents and an aunt. The aunt had legal custody of you at the time I found out about you," his mother explained to him. "We were living near Annapolis at the time. About a year and a half after we had adopted you, my friend told me your birth mother was thinking of taking you back again. She was going to re-marry and was having second thoughts."

Katherine stopped at this point and leaned back against the pillow, with a grimace and deep sigh.

Vern's father inserted himself into the conversation. "Maybe Vern's right, Katherine. I think we should wait until you're a little stronger to talk about this." He gave Vern a look that said, "Enough for now."

Vern took the signal and moved off the bed. "Dad's right. I want to hear all the details but only when you've had a few good meals under your belt. We need to pump you up a bit. You have a way to go yet before you're back to hiding presents under my bed."

They all laughed at that. His mother said, "Imagine that. We got away with it for two full years before you started imagining monsters under your bed and discovered the boxes." Katherine started with a coughing fit as she laughed so hard at the memory.

There was no stopping her. She had hidden this fact for so many years, and now she wanted to get it all out, to let Vern know how she and James had loved him so much. She continued with the story. "We were so afraid she'd hunt us down that we moved to Pennsylvania when we heard she might be changing her mind. It wasn't far. She probably could have searched for us. In those days you couldn't Google everything and everybody, so we felt safer at a distance."

"So, did you ever meet my mother? What about my father? Birth parents, I mean."

"No, I never knew her name or where she lived. My friend, Jenny, would never divulge the information, not even that of the aunt who had custody of you at the time."

51

"If she had custody, how were you able to adopt me?"

"By custody, I mean she was caring for you. It was more of a foster home the aunt was providing. She had a full house of her own. She had called social services to see about adoption. That's how Jenny knew about you." Katherine flushed, reluctant to go on.

"There's more." Vern sensed her hesitation. "So my aunt didn't want me either." He bit his lip before resuming. "Was I such a royal brat? Was I mean? Was I a liar? What was wrong with me?"

Tears flooded Katherine's eyes. "You must remember – you were a child, an innocent child. Of course there was nothing wrong with *you*. I never knew the details of your mother's life, but all I can say is there was definitely something wrong with *her*!"

Katherine continued with stories of Vern's childhood, times when they were about to tell him he was adopted, their fears that he'd want to be returned to his real mother. James added to the conversation with a joke about wanting to tell him when he was having so many problems assembling a bike, a train set, and a do-it-yourself work table one Christmas. "Your mother practically threw the table at me when I said that," he recalled. He looked down at Katherine and grinned at her. "You know it was only a joke, I hope," and then at Vern, "because I never ever wanted to give you up."

They told him how they were on tenterhooks for years after moving to the Tudor house in Wallingford. They cringed whenever a strange car pulled into the driveway, which was actually a mini-parking lot. Their home was the envy of the neighborhood. Now Vern wondered if his birth mother had been too poor to care for him. When his father opened his own insurance business, they could afford to give Vern all the material things he needed. Their life was one of daily thanksgiving for their son and their lifestyle. Vern could walk to school, and they could cross the street to the Country Club where they enrolled him in swimming lessons, eventually leading to membership on the swim team.

Vern's memory of walking home from school was not always the plus his parents thought it was. He recalled one time as a fifth grader he was chased by two tough kids from his class. In his later years he understood that they had suffered miserable lives at home. One's father was arrested for embezzling money and the other boy's parents divorced that same year. This was no consolation to him on that frightful day after a lesson on George Washington. They followed close behind him shouting to each other, "Let's mount Vernon!" They laughed the snarky laugh of bullies as they picked up stones from the side of the street and hurled them at Vern. The boys gained on him as he ran toward the Tudor house. He heard the taunts, "Go home, pig farmer. Go home and get your slops!"

The lesson that day had revealed that George Washington raised pigs at his Mount Vernon farm. The chance to ridicule Vern because of his name provided abundant entertainment for the toughs.

"Go get your slops your ma has stirred up!"

These were the last words Vern heard as he slipped between the hydrangea bushes on the way to the safety of his home. He leapt onto the patio and turned to face his pursuers. His heart pounded in his ears; he knew tears were forming. He wanted to run inside so they wouldn't see him cry, but he held his ground as they stood outside the yard and continued to hurl insults at him.

"Yeah, you're safe now. Maybe your mama will come out and throw some garbage to you, pig farmer!"

At that moment, his mother came to the patio door and stepped outside.

"Vern, what's going on here?" She looked toward the boys and called out, "Johnny, Mark, what's going on?"

"Nothing, Mrs. Alexander, we're just playin' with Vern," Johnny sang out. The boys looked uncomfortably at each other and murmured their agreement.

"Would you like to come in and have some snacks with us?" she asked.

Vern stiffened. He hoped they wouldn't be that bold. For a split second it looked like they would, but Johnny answered for the pair. "Thanks, but I have to walk the dog today." He looked toward Mark, who nodded that he, too, had chores to do.

"OK, maybe some other day." Mrs. Alexander smiled at them and touched Vern's shoulder to usher him into the house.

Once inside, Vern released his tension by launching an attack on his mother. "Why'd you have to name me a creepy name like Vernon? Where did that name pop up from?"

His mother was shocked by his anger. He had never questioned his name before. She gasped at the question.

"Well? Why did you give me that stupid name?"

She stammered, trying to find a suitable answer for the angry and frightened little boy. "Why is that a problem all of a sudden?"

He broke into tears as he explained the incident. She held him close but never explained the name. Now he realized why she couldn't explain it. Of course she hadn't chosen the name. He thought to himself that this was one of the many opportunities she had for telling him he was adopted, one of the many impossible moments that must have been a hundredfold.

Sitting next to his ailing and grief-stricken mother, he wondered if they had told him about the adoption earlier if he could have handled the Mount Vernon incident differently. Surely the boys would have done the same thing, but he would not have lashed out at his mother the way he did. On the other hand, he was only ten and maybe he would have lashed out at her for not changing the name when they adopted him. He patted her hand and said, "You had a tough time raising me. Thank you."

Katherine was visibly tiring. Her words came out more slowly, her breathing became labored, and she sank back again into her pillow.

"Mom. Let's give it a rest for a while," Vern said, as he tugged at his earlobe. He noticed how her eyes lit up at the suggestion. He wasn't sure if it was in defiance or in relief.

"Okay. I think I need a little nap now. I want to tell you so much, so many stories."

"I get the big picture," he said, "the main story. So you rest now." He settled the blankets around her frail frame, tucking them under her neck the way she did to him when he was a child.

The gesture did not go unnoticed. "Do you forgive me for holding this back?"

"Mom," he said, "there's nothing to forgive. Trust me. I can handle this. I can just imagine how hard it was for you all these years keeping it a secret."

He didn't realize when she smiled that she was remembering the words the night nurse had said: "Trust your son."

Chapter 5

I am part of the sun as my eye is part of me. That I am part of the earth my feet know perfectly, and my blood is part of the sea. My soul knows that I am part of the human race, my soul is an organic part of the great human race, as my spirit is part of my nation. In my own very self, I am part of my family.
David Herbert Lawrence, *Apocalypse*

VERN AND MARLA DROVE directly to the hospital on the return trip from the airport. As promised, she had retrieved his birth certificate from the safe deposit box. They discovered that it gave no significant information. "Vernon Thomas Alexander, parents James and Katherine Alexander, date of birth July 30, 1973. Place of birth Annapolis, Maryland. That's it – in total," she read aloud.

"Well, that's a start. I imagine the agency had that certificate issued with the adoption, but I'll bet there's an original with my birth parents' names on it somewhere." Vern looked at Marla as she slid the document back into its envelope. "Looks like the start of a quest, huh?"

She considered his remark in silence as they came closer to the hospital. "I guess you'll have to put that on hold a bit until your mom is out of the woods with this surgery that's coming up tomorrow."

"And the one after that – the big one." Vern pulled into the visitors' parking lot and drove around, finding the last available spot in that section. "Shall we walk from here, or do you want me to leave you off and meet you at the door?"

Marla was anxious to see her mother-in-law but happy to stall for a few extra minutes. Memories of her dying mother plagued her when she thought of Katherine lying in a hospital bed. Since the night they'd received the call about Katherine's hospitalization, Marla's dreams were filled with memories of her mother. She dreaded new memories of Vern's mom if she were to deteriorate and possibly die. "Let's walk. I'm ready to stretch my legs after sitting so long."

Katherine brightened when the two appeared in her doorway. The fact that James had just stepped out of the room lent itself to picking up sounds from the hallway. Their quiet voices signaled their arrival before they came into view. Vern poked his head around the doorframe first, followed close behind by Marla. "Here she is, fresh from the Delmarva Peninsula – Marla Alexander!" Vern announced.

Marla rushed to Katherine's bedside and reached for her mother-in-law. "I don't know where I can grab you," she said as she maneuvered her way through the remaining tubes.

"Grab me anywhere you want," Katherine said as she drew Marla as close to her as she could. They hugged for a long, intimate moment until Katherine sank back into her pillow. She looked up sadly at Marla. "I hope I haven't caused too much trouble for you and Vern with my news. I know he'll have told you."

Katherine was so small in the bed that she barely caused the blanket or sheets to form a mound. Marla felt around to establish the perimeters and then sat on the edge of the bed, being careful not to jostle her mother-in-law. "You're not the only one with a long held secret, you know. I guess it's high time I told *you* something."

Katherine looked at her with worry and curiosity burning in her eyes.

"You need to know that the only reason I married your son was that I wanted you as parents!" She smiled and took Katherine's hand as she told her this "secret."

Katherine grinned shyly. The impact of the message caused her to flush. She was not one who took compliments easily although she was quick to give them out. "Thank you for that."

"Really. Vern, didn't I used to tell you that?"

Vern stepped up to the pair. After hugging his mother, he confirmed that she had said that a few times during the rocky episodes with her father and brothers, along with doubts and fears about her mother's love for her. "Yeah, it really made me feel special that it wasn't my charming self that attracted her," he joked.

"You two," Katherine said, her voice hoarse, her eyes bright.

James returned to the room and lit up at the sight of Marla.

"See that?" Vern said. "I never get a smile like that. I believe the three of you have an admiration society that I'm not part of."

*****

Dinner was served to the other patients on the floor. The NPO sign had been returned to Katherine's chart. Her dinner came in the form of the drip coming from the tubes that were readying her for the ordeal in the morning. She sniffed the air and remarked, "A little canned gravy and some instant mashed potatoes would be a feast right now."

*****

That night, back at his parents' home, Vern and Marla sat down to some late night drinks. Vern told his father that they were putting off questions until Katherine was recovered. "I only have a few things I want to ask and that's it until Mom is better," he said.

"Vern, we both want to answer anything you might want to know. Your mother has made that clear, so fire away."

"Well, my birth certificate states that I was born in Annapolis. Is that true?

"No, Vern, you were actually born in Wisconsin, as far as we know. We never saw your original birth certificate. Apparently, that's where your grandparents lived."

"Then did I stay with them?"

"You and your mother stayed with them off and on, according to Jenny, before she moved to Maryland to be closer to her sister. Then she left you with her sister and took off again."

"Can you give me this Jenny's name? Maybe she can help me with some details."

"I'll get that information together for you. I hope your search doesn't lead to any disappointments."

Vern wondered if he meant his birth parents may have had a tainted past that would cause him to cast doubt upon himself. He hoped his father didn't think he would rather have had his original parents.

"Dad, the truth can never hurt," Vern offered.

*****

Marla had been hearing this mantra throughout their married life. Deep inside her, she felt that knowing who his birth parents were, no matter where it would lead, could do nothing but enrich his life. She said, "I know how much you and Mom have meant to Vern throughout his entire life. You chose to love him and raise him when you didn't have to. So many biological parents don't even *like* their children and make life miserable for them." She paused, choking up a little, as she remembered her father. "No matter where this search leads, it can never erase the beautiful memories the two of you have given him – and me."

She wondered what circumstances had led Vern's mother to give him up. Would he be heartbroken if he found out she was one of those loveless parents? Would he embrace this mother if he found out she was so

61

flawed that she had no personal resources, financially or emotionally, to love her child? From seeing his baby pictures – from the age of three and up – she knew how adorable he was. It had always been a mystery to her that the Alexanders did not have baby pictures from infancy to the age of three. How could a mother have abandoned that little boy?

She wondered if Vern, too, was thinking of the implications. How would he respond when he located his birth parents? Were they still alive? Did he have siblings? There were so many questions.

Chapter 6

Attempt the end, and never stand to doubt;
Nothing's so hard but search will find it out.
Robert Herrick, *Seek and Find*

KATHERINE'S SURGERY to implant the stents went smoothly. Marla and Vern returned to Fenwick Island to wait for the next step in her recovery. Vern returned to his computer business, concentrating more on his quest than his business. From the information his father gave him about Jenny, the social worker, he was able to apply for and receive documentation related to the adoption process from the State of Maryland.

"This is really an interesting account from the agency," he said to Marla one night after dinner. They had cleared the glass dining room table and laid the various reports out on top. Vern opened the file the caseworker had compiled. "A healthy, attractive child who has a nice sense of humor, is loyal and affectionate toward his family and has affected a happy adjustment," he read aloud to Marla. "Looks like James and Katherine really did set me up in the center of their life."

"In other words, you were a spoiled brat," she replied. She served his coffee with a deep bow.

"I guess I really was. It's funny how I completely blanked out on my former life... although there were moments as a teenager when things would happen. You know how people are always saying 'déjà vu?' Even now flashbacks occur sometimes, but I never thought of them as flashbacks, just curious moments."

"I've had them many times myself – I've heard it said that it's a physical phenomenon where the mind is catching up on the current status, like your brain has had a lapse or mini-stroke and is re-processing."

"Thanks a lot, Sigmund," Vern joked. "No, seriously – the name Pru keeps coming up in my déjà vu scenes. Scenes at the beach, scenes at French Creek Park in Pennsylvania, scenes around dinner tables." He blew at the steaming coffee and took a sip. As he eased a forkful of the Harris Teeter apple pie into his mouth, he brought back one such memory. "I see Pru now, laughing at me and wiping whipped cream or something off my nose. Her hands were so tender as she dabbed at me."

"That's funny," Marla said. "Maybe that's why you always are feeling around your nose when we have pumpkin pie or hot chocolate with whipped cream."

"Do I?" Vern was surprised at this observation. "I wonder if I have other mannerisms I adopted pre-Alexandrian days. And I wonder if I share them with any other relatives." He cocked his head and repeated, "Pre-Alexandrian, sounds like the Mesozoic Era or something. Or maybe I'm like Herb Philbrick and have led at least two lives, maybe even more…"

He went back to the report and read more about the separation from his natural parents. "Looks like Mommie Dearest shuttled me from pillar to post from one boarding house to another. Seems her first husband divorced her since she conceived me while he was sweating in the jungles of Vietnam. I must have been a funny welcome home present. Then the guy she hoped would be her second husband didn't want me." He frowned. When he looked toward Marla, he saw sympathy pouring from her. "I'm OK," he said.

He pored through the report trying to find information about the aunt who was caring for him when Katherine saw him at the restaurant. "Here's something," he said. "'Vernon was brought to Annapolis, Maryland, by his mother and placed with her sister where there were two children slightly younger and one slightly older.' It doesn't name her. She'll be the key, if I can find her."

"Maybe your Pru is the *slightly older* in your flashbacks."

*****

They decided to place an entry on his Facebook page. After scanning a picture of himself as a three-year-old, Vern posted it with this message:

Please help me find my cousin(s)

I was born July 30, 1973 in Wisconsin but spent some time near Annapolis, MD between 1974-1976. I believe I have three cousins, one whose name is Pru.

Do you recognize this little boy? I was about 3 years old when this picture was taken. Maybe you have other pictures of me.

Please like and share

He uploaded it to his Facebook page and posted it for general distribution. "I hope somebody sees it and responds," he said after looking it over on his home page. "We'll keep re-posting it until I find out something about my birth family."

Chapter 7

There is no more lovely, friendly and charming relationship,
communion, or company than a good marriage.
Martin Luther

TWO WEEKS LATER, when Vern made a last-minute check of his Facebook page before turning in for the night, he found a message.

It was from a Prudence Patterson. He checked her home page and examined the entries and photos. "I'm going to contact her," he told Marla, who looked over his shoulder as he scrolled through the pages.

"Do you think she's for real?" she asked as she fluffed the duvet and turned it down on her side of the bed. Their bedroom served as the office, too, the desktop computer sitting on a cherry worktable facing the Bay.

"Well, surely she's for real."

"But is she really your cousin, smarty pants?"

"I guess we'll see." He sent a note to her asking for contact information.

*****

A few days later Prudence sent her work address and this cryptic reply: *You need to come to Las Vegas. I have pictures and information that you will find invaluable. Please come alone.*

"Now what the hell does that mean?" Marla asked. "Have you suggested that you should call her and discuss this? Vern, this is really weird!"

They were seated across from each other in the dining area having a second cup of coffee after breakfast.

He scrolled back through the various messages on his Facebook page that had transpired and showed her where he had suggested the phone contact. "See, she doesn't want to put her phone number out there." He threw his hands up in resignation. "Do I write her off, or do I take the chance and check it out?"

"Can't she just send you the pictures?" Marla asked. She finished her cup of coffee and turned the laptop toward her, reading the message for the fifth time.

Marmalade leapt onto the table and padded his white–tipped feet across the keyboard. "Well, maybe there's your answer," Marla laughed. "He's telling you to strike her out."

"Well, kitty, I'm not taking your advice." He looked at Marla with his lips set in his *I'm not changing my mind* mode and said, "I've made a reservation for the Flamingo Hotel for next Wednesday and Thursday nights."

"What? And am I going with you?"

"No."

"Why can't I go?" Marla reached for her kitten and held it close, an action she had always taken with her previous cat, her armor against fear or disappointment. She shook her head back and forth and looked down, avoiding eye contact with Vern.

He wasn't sure what he should say. He also didn't tell her he had made telephone contact, that he'd messaged *his* phone number to her and that she had called *him*. Vern knew that he was betraying Marla's trust in this matter, but he didn't want to lose an opportunity to investigate this mysterious informant. He had scanned her Facebook page for information that might validate her claim. The telephone conversation had not been as helpful as he wanted. When he suggested she send copies of old photos similar to the one he'd posted, she insisted he should come to her and see the albums. He had told her he and Marla would come and combine the visit with a stay at a casino. This irritated her slightly. "She can't be here when you find out what I have to tell you," she had said.

Why can't I go? Her question deserved to be answered. But how could he tell her he had talked to Pru when he had already said she wanted no phone contact?

"Well, I thought it better to go alone and save your sick leave days for when we have to go back to Florida."

He knew she would see his eyes narrow as he made this flimsy excuse, so he directed his gaze downward at the computer screen.

Marla squirmed in her chair, the slight motion causing the cat to jump down from her lap. She twisted her ring, an action she always resorted to when nervous. "I don't know, Vern. This seems pretty fishy to me. Let me get another look at this woman." She motioned for the laptop. She studied the home page of Prudence Patterson, looking for links to Vern's past. "She's a bombshell, to be sure, but I don't see any connections to Maryland or Wisconsin. I do see that she works at the Flamingo." She looked up at Vern, who was directing his attention toward the deck.

"Anything wrong with that?" he asked. "That's why I'm staying there – so I can avoid going to her home with all this cat and mouse stuff." As he said it, he knew there was definitely something wrong with excluding Marla from this visit, but he was afraid Prudence was about to divulge some family secret that might be embarrassing. "Besides, maybe she'll tell me something we might not want to know."

"*We* is the operative word here, Vern. There can be nothing *we* can't face together. You've spent your whole life not even knowing these people. What can she possibly say that is enough for you to bear and not worthy of sharing with me?" She left the table, gathering her plates, and put them in the dishwasher. "I have to leave for work." Normally she kissed him before leaving, but this time she simply paused behind him as she prepared to check last minute details and get her school supplies. She pointed to the Facebook page and said almost inaudibly, "This really hurts."

He knew she'd be hurt. He knew how much trust they put in each other, how they shared everything. Except this. He knew the allure was not that Prudence was the bombshell Marla detected, but what was he trying to do, why this secrecy? Was he trying to protect Marla from a scurrilous family history? His rational mind knew that no past actions could hurt them, even if his father had been a direct descendant of John Wilkes Booth or Adolph Hitler or any notorious character. Even if his father sat in Rikers Island, or his mother, for that matter, it would not impact on their lives. Or would it? What would be the greater disaster here – Pru's information or the betrayal of Marla? Would she ever get over the fact that he had gone forward without her? Would she always question his actions in the future whenever a difference of opinion came up?

Why can't I go? He didn't want to cross Prudence, that's why. Unknown Prudence. Stranger Prudence. Maybe Cousin Prudence.

*****

Marla had been cool to him since the conversation at the breakfast table when he'd announced his plans to meet Prudence. She did not believe she needed to be protected and did not believe he needed to go during the week when she could not leave school. She told him that it was a stretch to decide for her that she needed to save her days off when a weekend would have required either no days or, at the most, one day of leave. She had plenty of sick days accumulated and would have had no qualms about being "sick" to accompany him.

He had seen her on her computer checking out Prudence Patterson. Some of her photos were pretty racy - sexy poses with pouty lips and skimpy clothing. In fact, he thought she looked rather slutty and imagined Marla thought the same. Marla had asked him the same haunting question at least three times since that day:

Why can't I go? Only – she followed it with remarks like "Are you attracted to her?" "Would I cramp your style?" "Are you having a mid-life crisis?" None of the questions carried a tinge of humor. They were all sharp and stinging.

All day at work, Vern pondered Marla's question, *Why can't I go?* He called the airlines and the hotel and cancelled the trip. He knew he had to talk this out with her. On the way home from work, he bought a bouquet of yellow roses and lilies from the Bethany Florist Shop and placed them in the center of the table. The warm spring air wafted in from the deck as he stood out there, thinking of how they would have the conversation about this mission.

*****

He heard the key downstairs in the lock as Marla opened the door. She trudged up the steps, toting her portfolio of student artwork. She's got a lot on her plate today, he thought, as he came into the dining room from the deck. She was at the landing by the kitchen door when he saw her spot the flowers. He expected her face to light up the way it always did when she was happy. But her smile didn't erupt.

Instead, she said, "I guess this is supposed to make me forget that you're going off to see the mystery woman." The pain in her face showed as she put her portfolio down and turned toward the hall to the bedroom.

"Wait, Marla." He hurried toward her as she continued on her way. "Please."

She ignored him and continued down the hall.

"I've cancelled the trip," he said softly.

With that, she turned toward him and came back into the living room.

"We need to talk. Come, let's sit here." He motioned to the sectional sofa. They sat with one cushion between them, the hurt still on her face, but a warm spark in her eyes coming through. "Can I get you something to drink? You look pretty beat today."

"Will I need a drink?" she asked, the uncertainty returning.

"No, not really, but I think I have a lot of explaining to do. I know how deeply you felt about your mother's death - and how I lacked a complete understanding of that, how it put a wedge between us until you let me in on it." He looked at her as though begging for forgiveness. "You made me see just how deep that whole thing was." He paused, looked out on the deck at a pair of cardinals, and dimpled. "Remember how you said those cardinals were closer to each other than we were then?"

She nodded and flushed slightly in recognition.

"Well, I'm not going to be responsible for another wedge. I don't know if you know just how deep this desire goes - to know who my birth parents are. I love, without question, my real parents, but I want to get to know who these other people are." He scratched the back of his neck. "How could my birth mother give me away? What kind of a woman was she? Who was my birth father? Certainly not the man she was married to." His brow furrowed. He clenched his teeth. He knew as

Marla patted his leg and moved closer to him that she saw his pain.

"You know your whole family history, for better or worse," he continued. "Even though your father and brothers are dicks, we know who they are and can choose to invite them to events or not. You know where your green eyes came from; you know to have a mammogram done each year given your mother's history. But I don't have any of that." He looked down at his hands. "That's no excuse for me planning this trip without telling you." He looked straight into her eyes. "I don't ever want to hurt you. I just got caught up in it. I even lied about the telephone contact and that hurts me maybe more than it hurts you." He saw the flash of surprise turn to pain in her eyes when he admitted that. "I sent her my number and we've talked three times.

"There's so much missing in my past now that I know there is a whole set of relatives out there somewhere. You've seen picture albums from the day you came home from the hospital. We always wondered where my baby pictures were. When my parents told me some boxes went missing when they moved, I always thought my pictures were in those boxes."

Marla looked toward the hall and the steps leading to the front door. "Right," she said. "We always wondered why the one of you with your shark and the one in the sailor outfit were the first records of you."

He twisted his earlobe and continued, "So, when this Prudence contacted me, it was like a giant opening. When I told her we would come and she told me to come alone, I wanted so much to get the information that I freaked, I guess. At first I thought I'd do it her way, that maybe you needed to be protected from some terrible family secret. But the truth is, I don't even know if she *is* my cousin and if she is, I know whatever she has to say, we have to face together."

The kitten leapt onto the couch and inserted himself between the two. Marla took him in her lap and edged closer to Vern, "He's always a little comic relief. And we needed some relief, to be sure." She petted Marmalade and released him when his ears perked up as he spotted two squirrels on the deck.

"Why do you think Prudence insisted on *alone*? And if I should come with you, what can she do? Refuse to talk to you?" She thought about that for a minute. "And if she does, we could just make a vacation of it."

"Good points - all of them."

"We need a vacation anyway. It's been a long, tough winter. Now that spring is in the air, and my spring break is coming up, we can stay for three or four days and see the sights, take in some shows."

They hashed out several scenarios, all of which had to include Vern's mother and the what if's, along with the impending amount of time he'd need to spend in Florida. The implant of the stents had been very successful. She was gaining back weight and felt so much better, but the tumor still needed to be removed. In the end, they decided that they would go to Las Vegas together for two days as he'd originally allotted to the visit.

Marla hoped it would prove worthwhile.

Fran Hasson

Chapter 8

Canst thou not minister to a mind diseased,
Pluck from the memory a rooted sorrow,
Raze out the written troubles of the brain,
And with some sweet oblivious antidote
Cleanse the stuffed bosom of that perilous stuff
Which weighs upon the heart?
William Shakespeare, *Macbeth*

THEY BEGAN THE TRIP to the Philadelphia International Airport for the flight to Vegas a week later than the original plan. The same attendant was on duty as he reached out for the ticket to the remote lot. He wondered if the beefy man remembered the hanging gas cap. Vern reflected that his lapse with the cap was nothing compared to the lapse he almost created by putting aside Marla's needs. He remembered thinking that his forgetfulness couldn't be impending dementia since his parents had no such signs. But did his birth parents?

He colored a bit when he thought about the mysterious Prudence and felt ashamed that he had even considered leaving Marla at home to make the trip. Marla was right – What could she possibly have to say that his wife couldn't hear? Nevertheless, a nagging voice inside taunted, What makes me think Prudence wants anything more than to help me out?

*****

At the airport in Las Vegas, they negotiated their way from the arrivals gate to the ground transportation, gawking at the myriad slot machines throughout the terminal. "They don't have this many slots at Dover Downs!" said Marla. "Shall we try our luck?" She hesitated in front of one of her favorites, Double Diamonds.

"I think we'd better stick to trying our luck at the Flamingo, both with the slots and with Prudence," answered Vern, as he took her elbow and gently steered her toward the exit. She kept looking back at the machines and frowning at Vern as they made their way to the ground transportation.

The ride on the shuttle bus seemed to overwhelm Marla. She remarked about how surprised she was that it looked so common. "I was expecting lights, camera, action," she said. The route to the casinos took them past boarded-up buildings, liquor stores, wooden fences covered with spray-painted graffiti, groups of young people leaning against rusted chain link fences passing spliffs to each other. They could almost smell the pot through closed windows of the bus. "This looks absolutely squalid!"

"I don't remember it being this run down. You'll see what you're expecting when we get to the Strip." Vern hadn't been to Vegas in a long time and was surprised himself to see so many new casinos replacing the old stand-bys he had seen or read about: the Sands, Dunes, and Flamingo; now the new Flamingo, Bellagio, Caesar's Palace, and a bevy of high-rise, mega-glittered casinos prevailed. They were connected by a monorail along the new Strip.

Their shuttle left them between Margaritaville and the main entrance of the Flamingo. Strains of *Cheeseburger in Paradise* boomed from the open entrance. "Let's go in this way," Vern said. They followed the small afternoon crowd into the tropical bar. "Tonight you'll see the wonder of it all when all the lights stand out." They proceeded through the bar area to the hotel foyer, slots zinging and pinging, through to the promenade and its line of gift shops from *Sex and the City* to coffee bars. "You know what?" asked Vern. Without waiting for Marla's answer, he continued. "For a minute, I forgot why we were here!"

*****

After checking in and freshening up, they came back down to the main section of the casino. The flashing lights and clanging of the one-arm bandits would cause seizures in some, but most people were oblivious to the noise, in fact relished it, the stimulation being the only action many had in their lives. Vern was attuned to the demand of the raucous sounds. His world was one of computers, so his attention was devoted to the working of the electronics, the rhythmic whirring, the metallic noise produced when patrons cashed out their winnings. He knew how they created that sound, how they heightened its noise to make those around the seemingly fortunate gambler think the lucky winner was collecting bucketsful of money, how this was just another commercial gimmick.

Marla was mesmerized by all the color, her artist's mind comparing the psychedelic colors to those found in nature. She watched the animated gremlins, sharks, orcs, and mummies race across the screens, and thought of her students and their love of computer graphics. Despite her youth, which to her students was actually old age, Marla was pretty much old school. She loved the Italian Renaissance painters - the details of hands, noses, faces, so painstakingly rendered by the masters. She equally adored the Impressionists with their hints of those same features. She definitely was not one who preferred to illustrate with the *anime* characters the students loved so much and were evident in many of the games, but she was, nevertheless, entranced by them.

They scanned the floor, seeking out the Blackjack tables. Marla saw Vern's eyes lingering longer at each section, thoroughly tracking each machine, each table, each blonde-haired woman in the crowd. Marla cut to the chase. She had memorized each facet of Prudence Patterson from her copious photos on Facebook. Her eye for detail was honed; she did not need the careful consideration which Vern gave everything. She found Prudence while Vern was still scouring the Roulette and neighboring Blackjack tables. She looked older than the pictures, but her straight back, ample bosom, and swept-back hair were discernible as the cousin Vern sought, the one plastered all over her Facebook page. Her heart pounded. "There she is," she said to Vern as she twisted her ring, then grabbed his elbow and motioned with her head.

"Great! Let's go over there." Vern was straight up, ready to face all challenges, first in line at the ski lift, first to volunteer at the magic shows, first to plunge into a new business of his own without any fear of failure.

"Don't you want to watch her for a while?" asked Marla, her reticent nature taking hold. She wanted to examine this woman, this intruder in their lives who would have separated them for this venture into the unknown, this would-be cousin who held such deep dark secrets she didn't want Vern to bring her along.

"I don't want to watch her; I want to talk to her. Are you coming or not?" he asked. Vern was an attack dog while Marla was more of a bloodhound. He scented his quarry and wanted to spring upon it while Marla wanted to sniff all around the perimeter before letting out her long howl, announcing her discovery.

"Do you think I should go with you or wait over here at one of the slots?"

Vern stepped back, cocked his head, and took a long look at Marla. "You're afraid, aren't you?"

Her mouth puckered a little and she hunched her shoulders, held her elbows close and screwed up her lips. "I guess so. I guess maybe she wanted you here alone for a reason. Maybe I should have let you come by yourself."

"Nonsense - come on. When I told her I was bringing you and that was that, she gave in without a fight."

Marla reluctantly let Vern guide her to the Blackjack table. They sat at the end closer to Pru's left hand. She observed silently as the woman's hands deftly spread the cards across the surface when they emerged from the eight-deck "shoe." She smoothed them left and right, carefully positioning them so their totals showed clearly. She watched the bettors place their chips and nodded toward the participants. When she was sure they were all ready, she turned over her card. Marla noticed how some of the men were paying as much attention to Prudence's cleavage as to the operation of the cards. Not diehard gamblers, she thought. These were the men Prudence eyeballed intensely as she leaned forward, her top two buttons open and promising more than the cards would give.

She could almost hear the whirring in the others' brains as they counted aces and tens. Vern had told her in advance about card counting, something he liked to try himself but a trick that would never occupy her time. She'd rather paint pictures of the players, the detached dealer with graceful hands floating over the pink felt surface, the glazed eyes of the gawkers, the passionate concentration of the card sharks. She thought of how she would convey this in a drawing and conjured up images of the famous Coolidge paintings of dogs playing poker. Maybe that would be the best way because she didn't think she could capture the minds that were processing like computers unless she could snap some candid shots to freeze the tight lips, the narrowed eyes, the bent heads that avoided the dealer's eyes, hiding their intent when she looked their way. She glanced over at Vern and saw that determined look on his face as though *he* were counting cards, and shot an elbow at him. "Be careful," she whispered. "You'll get us banned."

As Pru's eyes scanned the crowd of players, they rested on Marla and Vern. "Care to play?" she asked.

"Do we know each other?" Vern asked, looking at the name tag that claimed she was Sherry.

"Come back to the entrance to Margaritaville at nine," she said softly, leaning forward to sweep the chips from the previous deal. She turned to the players and watched as the next round of chips mounded higher at the places of the vigilant men who gaped at her open bodice.

As they waited for nine o'clock to come, they drank margaritas near the entrance to the Jimmy Buffet lounge. "You keep referring to her as Prudence and I keep calling her Pru," Vern remarked. "I always hear this little voice in my flashback saying *Pru*. I wonder what she calls herself."

"Obviously Sherry," Marla returned. "And I really don't think she is very prudent, so I guess I'll call her Pru, too."

"Now why do you say she's not very prudent? You don't even know her."

"Yes, I do. I'm willing to bet a lobster dinner when we get home that she has no female friends," Marla said, her chin jutting forward the way it always did when she was stock sure of herself. "Did you notice the way the

83

flamingos on her button covers were practically pecking at her nipples?"

Vern laughed but did not answer, instead licked the salt from the rim of his glass and smirked at her as he looked toward the casino floor. "Hmmm, here comes our little bombshell now."

The meeting was short and sweet as Pru had only a half-hour dinner break. They made plans to meet the next day. "I have off tomorrow, so I'll meet you at the little pizza place by the elevators. I'll take you to my place and we'll go over my albums and see if I'm who you're looking for. And if you're who I think you are. Things seem to fit into place and I think we are cousins." She grinned what seemed a genuine smile of warmth that made Marla feel guilty and made her think of where she would be taking Vern for the lobster dinner.

*****

Pru drove the two to her apartment. The route to her place took them past shoddy buildings, unkempt neighborhoods, and ramshackle homes. Thin dogs snuffled around dumpsters; the streets were dusty and full of litter; hand-lettered signs advertised rooms for rent and cheap sex. The worn and rugged mountains in the distance buffered the unattractiveness of the streets they were passing. The few people hanging about looked ragged, poorly dressed; mothers were pulling children down the street, cars were prowling slowly and drivers were looking sinister as though trolling for unaware tourists. Vern thought of his mother and how, when she'd see a woman dragging her child, she'd want to go over and shake such mothers. He had the urge to get out of the car and do the same. He thought of Las Vegas as the City of Sin; how strange that his search had brought him to this place where he hoped to discover the secret of his birth mother's sin. Which was her greater sin – the adulterous affair that led to his birth or the rejection of him? It seemed to him the appropriate setting for whatever revelation awaited.

They took the elevator to the top floor of the ten-story faded pink building and emerged to sour cooking smells, apparently trapped in the narrow corridor for years and absorbed into the graying walls. It was obvious that no painting or upkeep was part of the lease. Bare walls and threadbare carpeting were the welcoming committee. Vern and Marla cast wary glances at each other. He felt the impulse to call everything off, hail a taxi, and return to Fenwick Island. Fresh odors of tomatoes and sausage overpowered the ancient smells that had assaulted their noses.

"It seems Maria Cruz is at it today. Sometimes the smells coming from there make me want to break down her door and run off with what's on the stove," Pru said.

"Does she ever invite you over?" asked Marla.

"I wouldn't go if she did."

Vern and Marla looked at each other. "Why not?" asked Vern. "Is she some kind of nut?"

Pru's eyes rolled and she glanced disgustedly toward the Cruz's apartment and said, "I'm not of her culture."

Vern wondered what she meant by that and was becoming more unsettled with this so-called cousin. He wondered if she really were his cousin. What kind of upbringing did she have that she was so condescending? She, too, lived in this rundown neighborhood, not exactly where the social structure exuded class, wealth, and a rich sophistication. He didn't want to give off any signals with his body language that he was leery of her, but he stared at her, watching her eyerolling accompanied by a twisting of the head and rolling of the shoulders. He detected a small spasm of her chin as she unlocked the door and ushered them into her apartment.

"Welcome to my home," she said and swept her arm signaling them to have a look. "It ain't much, but it's what I have. I'll give you the Cook's tour first; then we'll get down to business." At this, she nodded toward the stack of photo albums on the packing crate that served as a coffee table.

The apartment was small but laid out well. It smacked of the 60's, the avocado appliances and speckled formica counters in the kitchen sitting atop chipped and worn linoleum that needed replacement and was revealing the concrete floor below it.

Wow," said Marla, "how have you kept those appliances going? Aren't they from the 60's?"

Pru's face tightened in response to what Vern thought she might perceive as an insult since Marla's voice had conveyed that edge that was sometimes mistaken as criticism. He had often told her she had a teacher's voice, a reprimand complicit with that tone. "Actually, this complex was built at the end of the avocado run – the mid-80's. I'll have to replace those antiques soon, but I guess you can tell the slumlord here doesn't think too much of his tenants. So I don't know if he'll pay for them." She went to the door and hitched up the series of locks running along the frame.

After going through the one-bedroom unit and admiring the view from "the penthouse," they headed toward the wood frame sofa to sit before the stacks of photos. Marla hesitated between the bedroom and living area, taking in the panorama below. The worn and aged Rockies, although they shared some of the characteristics of Pru's apartment, added a majesty to the scene. Their craggy summits and hidden secrets seemed to relieve the shabbiness and poverty evident in Pru's humble existence. "I can see why you moved here," she said to Pru. "Your placement of your bed and I guess your favorite chair in the living room must give you a peaceful feeling every time you are at home and look out at this view."

Vern breathed a sigh of relief as he saw Pru's tense shoulders relax. He thought it must be a little embarrassing for her to show off her meager surroundings. He settled onto one of the faded blue cushions. There were six pieces - three backs and three seats, all padded with foam and all showing signs of wear with the edges fraying and sections of the crumbling insides protruding. The favorite chair Marla had mentioned was the bright spot of this room, the latest model La-Z-Boy chestnut leather recliner that looked like it swiveled and rocked.

The colorful painting hanging over it of Las Vegas Boulevard had to have been a very pricey piece, one that also eased the dinginess of the tiny apartment. Vern saw the approval in Marla's eyes as they rested on the painting. She stood before the painting, admiring it. He knew she'd be tracing the brush strokes, assessing it for the placement of the buildings, the traffic snaking past the most famous casinos, the skyline bright with the setting sun and the many colors in the sky resting on the Eiffel Tower, illuminating the Flamingo, coloring the fountains at the Bellagio. She was in a world of her own.

Pru noticed the rapt attention Marla was giving the painting but ignored her and went to the stack of photo albums. She sat down, put her hand on a cushion, and patted it as a signal for Vern to come closer. The two began looking through the books. Marla joined them when she heard Vern asking for the oldest ones.

Pru handed him a black imitation leather book with gold gilded patterns around three sides. Yellowed edges of old faded color photographs were peeling away from where the missing black angled corners used to be. The edges curled over and Vern pressed them down, looking for the little blond-haired boy.

There he was - climbing on Pru's tiny back! She was not much bigger than he was. "That's me, isn't it?" he said to Pru. "It looks like my picture I put on Facebook." He was amazed that Pru seemed to have a pictorial history of the pre-Alexandrian days he and Marla had talked about.

"Of course," she said. "That's why I replied. I got these albums out as soon as I saw your posting." She tugged at her left earlobe and twisted it.

"Vern," Marla said, "look at her ear."

Vern was ready to be vexed with Marla at this inappropriate remark but his gaze went first to Pru's ear, an automatic response. He tugged at *his* left ear, a motion he often made when a little nervous and twisted it.

The action made Pru break into a grin. "OK, cousin, I guess that does it."

They each examined the other's ears while Marla watched with tears forming in her eyes. "Your little heart-shaped earlobes, the earlobes next to your hearts - definitely in your DNA!" Marla said as she sat on the third cushion, joining them as they leafed through the album.

"That's my mother," Pru said. "She took you in several times when Aunt Grace was on the move."

"Grace – so that's my mother's name?"

"Yes, here she is – one of the rare photos I have of her. I don't recall a whole lot about what was going on those days. You can see from this picture. My mother is holding you and I'm holding my mother's skirt. I just about reach her hips. I guess you were about two and I was about five years old in this shot." She turned the page, looking for more pictures of Vern's mother, finding one on the last page. In that color snapshot, she was standing next to a slim man who was a little shorter than she was. They were standing in front of a Volkswagen. "They had just bought the car. I remember her fawning all over it – her first new car ever. They took me for a ride, told me it could go like a rabbit. I found out later that's what it was – a VW Rabbit!"

"So that's my father?" Vern asked. He looked hard for a family resemblance, poring over every detail from his straight combed-back hair to his bony hands that didn't look much bigger than his mother's to his baggy pants that seemed too big for his small frame. "I think the Rabbit came out in the late 70's. I don't remember ever seeing it or riding in it." He looked over at Marla and said, "I guess because by that time I was with my parents, the Alexanders."

"That I can't tell you," answered Pru. "I'm not sure she was married to that guy right then." There was a condescension in her tone. He wasn't sure whether it was directed at his mother or the man standing next to her. He recalled reading in the social worker's account that Grace dumped him one time when the man she wanted to marry insisted she had to let him go. He was dispensable whenever having him around was inconvenient. Was this the man she eventually married?

When they finished with that album, which Pru said was the only one with pictures that would feature Vern, he asked her if he could borrow any of the pictures and if she would give him his mother's name so he knew what to ask for in trying to secure his birth certificate. He also wanted her mother's information and that of his cousins. Clearly excited to know he had a family, his face beamed as he asked for these details. "I want to find out everything I can. Sooner than later," he added.

Pru gave them scant information: she didn't want to give out her sisters' and brother's names and addresses or her mother's address. She said it would take some research to get information about his mother. He wasn't sure he believed her version of this and was unsettled when she looked around the apartment at her shabby belongings and said to him, "I've had a pretty rough time of it. My family and I aren't real close. Other people seem to get support when there's hard times, but my folks haven't helped me much. Maybe you can help me out a little and I can help you find your mother, my Aunt Grace."

Vern and Marla looked at each other. He saw a little glint of anger fire her eyes and figured she was saying, "I knew she was trouble." He knew Marla had distrusted Pru ever since she had insisted he come alone. Even though he had changed the plans and included her, she would not forget Pru's attempt to keep her out of it. Now he was realizing why Pru wanted him to come alone and Marla probably was, too.

"Let me get this straight," he said. "Do you mean you want me to pay you for this *research*?"

"Well, I'm not sure I'd quite put it that way," she said. "We're family. Let's just say you could help me and I could help you. It's obvious," she said as her eyes settled on Marla's Louis Vuitton rose pink handbag, "that you're pretty well off. I originally thought you should come alone because it would be cheaper for you, but it didn't seem to be a problem to buy two airline tickets at the last minute."

Marla clutched her bag as Pru stared at it. It had been the most expensive Christmas gift Vern had ever purchased for her and had cost him the profits from at least ten computer repairs. Vern could see the tension building up in Marla's face and flinched as she inserted herself into the conversation. "Or maybe you could have put the pressure on Vern better if he were alone," she added. Her chin was tilted upward with her "high and mighty" pose, as Vern called it. He knew she had every right to come back at Pru; under ordinary circumstances she was not so defensive and confrontational, but he wished she would have remained quiet. Marla had a strong sense of right and wrong, fairness and cheating, loyalty and treachery. He hoped the two women would be able to restrain themselves. If they would never like each other, he hoped he could at least calm them both down and get the information he wanted. He knew Marla understood the importance of this visit and trusted that his penetrating stare would hold her back until they were alone.

Pru twisted her earlobe again. She pressed her lips together as she glared briefly at Marla, then recklessly pushed the photo albums back on the shelves under the window. She turned to Vern and said coolly, "I'll take you back to the hotel now and you two can think about what you want to do."

Marla was becoming more agitated. As Vern sensed the growing anger and obvious tension growing between the two women, he asked, "How much will your *research* cost?"

Marla's face reddened. "Vern," she said, "can't we just get this information ourselves – on our own?" She scowled at Pru and directed her next comment to her. "Maybe this is why your family hasn't helped you. Anyway, I thought dealers at the tables made pretty good money. Why are you doing this to us?"

This irritated Pru to the next level. She slammed the final photo album onto the top shelf and wheeled around, facing the two. She said to Vern, "Look, cuz, it's simple. Either I help you or I don't. I'll give you my mother's information for a thousand bucks and you can take it from there – or leave it. It's up to you."

Vern was startled. He looked at Marla, who seemed more than startled. He could see the hair on the back of her neck hackling like their kitten's back when he wanted to attack the mourning doves on their deck. He almost expected her to chatter her teeth the way Marmalade did at such times. She leaned forward on the couch and looked ready to spring. He decided it was time to let her know unequivocally that he wanted to handle this himself. He touched her arm and nudged her back into her seat.

"First of all," he said to Pru, "do you really think that's reasonable? Second, why not give me *my* mother's address? Why *your* mother?"

He watched Pru process the questions. The spasm in her chin that he had seen earlier increased, became a tic. Her head tilted with each movement of the chin. She was clearly becoming more agitated. He wondered if she kept a gun in the apartment because the crazed look that she directed at him and Marla was a bit frightening. He stood and walked toward her, his palms upright in a pose of submission, reaching as though he wanted to hug her. In a quiet voice he said, "You know, over the years I've had these kind of flashbacks and you were always in them – Pru at the playground, Pru at French Creek State Park where that photo shows all of us, Pru wiping whipped cream off my nose." She allowed him to touch her arm gently. "There was never a Pru like this. You're practically asking for extortion money. I'm shocked."

She backed away from him, frowned at Marla, and answered. "Look around here. I'm not living at a seashore resort. This is Sin City and it doesn't come cheap and the livin' ain't easy, not like with Porgy and

Bess. I guess you can say I been rode hard and put up wet, very different from your lives. So like I said, take it or leave it. I gotta do what I gotta do. You and the Princess can think it over and decide what you want to do."

"A thousand dollars?" asked Marla. "Really, Pru, do you know how hard we work for our money?" She was using a conciliatory tone. She knew Vern would disapprove, but she wanted to be a second voice of reason in this stand-off.

"I really don't care," Pru answered. "Let's go now. You can call me when you've decided."

"Wait, Pru. Please," said Vern. "We came here not to get into an argument with you or have bad feelings. I'm just interested in finding my birth parents. Do you really feel the need to extort money from me for this?" He motioned toward her recliner. "Can't you sit down and we'll just talk about this a bit?"

He looked sidelong toward Marla, who was twisting her ring and gritting her teeth. She squirmed at the edge of her seat, still clutching her handbag. He knew she was smarting from the dig about her bag and that she'd take a while to calm down. He hoped she wouldn't insert herself into the conversation again.

He touched Pru's arm again and led her to her chair. There was a small ottoman next to the chair, piled with magazines and mail. "Do you mind?" he asked as he reached toward the pile. She shrugged and he placed the pile on the coffee table and sat next to her.

"Maybe it would have been better if I'd come alone," he started, looking over at Marla apologetically. "Maybe you feel threatened because there are two of us here, like two against one?" He noticed Marla relax and lean back into her seat. He knew she'd have been furious if he made her out to be a barrier to this cousins' reunion. "But Pru, there's no two against one or any battle going on here. I love my wife and share everything with her. I'm so sorry that your life has developed this way, that you have no family encouragement, no one to back you up. Maybe I shouldn't even pursue this search for my parents. Maybe they're really bad people for me to get tied up with."

She seemed calmer, the tightness around her mouth slackened, her shoulders relaxed, the angry look gone from her eyes. She remained silent, so Vern continued, telling her of his upbringing, of the love his parents had given him, of the privileges he had enjoyed. He told her that they knew he was searching for his birth parents and that his mother was dying of pancreatic cancer, that she wanted to help him and had given him all the information she had about his past, but the missing information was so important to him.

"Do you think it will make your life better to know your real parents?" Pru asked.

"James and Katherine Alexander are my real parents. I just am curious about my family connections. Maybe health issues, maybe siblings and relatives I can invite to family reunions...." He stopped at this point and looked over at Marla, flashing a mischievous smile. He directed a comment to his wife. "We have no family reunions at this time, do we? But we'd like to."

Vern saw Marla manage a smirk, and he wondered if she was reading his thoughts – that the reason was because her father and brothers were pretty disgusting. He knew, however, that they could say what they wanted about their family, but that it was beyond the limits to let a stranger such as Pru in on it. He wanted to lessen some of the tension that had developed between Marla and Pru and felt that making Marla somewhat vulnerable would give Pru an edge she needed at this point. But he was afraid to make that point. "Now I do have a family and I'd like to get to know them."

"Well, now you do, but I might not be invited to your family reunion," Pru said. She looked around her apartment. "See this chair I'm sitting on? It took me some real degrading stuff to get this. And the painting?" It was the one Marla had looked at earlier. From her spellbound attention, Vern figured she had assessed it as an original, expensive at that. "A night of rolling around with a tourist. He had it in his room and insisted I should take it. No, I don't think you'd want me at your reunions."

"How about if you let us make the decision as to who's on our guest list?" Vern said as he took her hands into his.

Hers were sweaty and cool. She started to pull them back, but after looking into his cobalt eyes, she relaxed her hands and smiled slightly. "Your eyes are so familiar. I'm trying to think who in our family has such kind and gentle eyes. It's not a dominant trait."

He had obviously won her confidence. "What? The blueness or the kindness," he joked. "Seriously, I'm happy to have found you ... or should I say that you've found me."

Pru interrupted. "I think we've found each other." She stared into his eyes as though trying to grasp his soul, so intense was she. Finally she said softly, "I'm sorry to have been such a prig about asking for money..."

He sensed her sudden humility and embarrassment and broke into her conversation. "Look, Pru, we *are* family and now is the time to start acting like it. I want to know the rest of the family and find out where I fit in. I'll be glad to give you the money you asked for, but I'd prefer to give it to you as a gift, not as payment for information."

Pru regained her composure. "Vern, I'll call my mother and give her your information. I'm not sure she even knows where her sister is. The whole family is fucked up, not just me. But I think it starts with your mother. If they're not speaking, I wouldn't be surprised if my mom just got tired of all the drama."

"What if your mother won't give me the information? Do you think she'll contact me?"

"When I said I get no support from my family, I was a little unfair. Let's just say I'm out of the loop when it comes to family matters. The only one who talks to me is my mother. Not that my brother and sisters don't talk, but we've lost touch over the years." She scanned her surroundings, shaking her head as though she reflected nothing but failure. "But there's always Mom - Mother's love, you know how that is - unconditional love and all that horseshit." She colored a bit, realizing why Vern was there and that he must be thinking – *not my mother* - . "Anyway, she keeps in touch with me more than I do with her. I think I'm an embarrassment to the family. But my mother is a good person. She'll contact you for sure, and she'll help you if she can."

Chapter 9

Beware of allowing a tactless word, a rebuttal
a rejection to obliterate the whole sky.
Anaïs Nin, *The Diary*

WHEN THEY WERE AIRBORNE, he leaned back into
the seat and thought about why he would want to know a
family whose first representative was the unethical
cousin Pru, the little girl who featured strongly in his
memories, fond memories of his past. What had
happened to her over the years? He hoped the thousand
dollars they had picked up at the American Express
office would go to a good cause, make her life just a
little easier for the time being. He actually felt sorry for
Pru that she'd had to grovel in this way for money. It
was obvious that she needed financial help. What had
she done with her life? She was older than he and was
living in such a downtrodden environment. Was there no
one in her life she could turn to? Did she have a drug or
alcohol problem? How had she ended up so bitter and
defeated? The whole thing about the Cruz family not of

her culture, the worn furniture and dilapidated apartment, the seedy neighborhood. The money wasn't a big problem for Vern and Marla. They had two incomes, no children, and a very thriving business. He wondered if he'd keep in touch with Pru and try to help her in the future. He looked over at Marla playing Words with Friends on her iPad and decided not to mention that to her. She was stabbing the letters with a vengeance and he wondered if she was re-living the encounter with Pru.

*****

Vern opened the door to his computer shop and breathed in the refreshing scent of running motors, plastic cords, and day-old coffee being re-heated in the back room. Ah, home at last, he thought and went into the work area. His assistant, Jared, was hunched over a table peering into the inner workings of a desktop computer as it hummed and burned. "I guess that's what I smelled when I came in," Vern said, startling the worker. He stood behind and watched as Jared tilted the machine.

He switched it off and went for the duster on a shelf behind the table. "Just what I thought," he said. "This whole fan is coated with dust and dirt." He directed the spray at the inner workings.

"Good job, Jared. It made my trip so much easier to know you were here and able to take care of everything." He walked around looking at the desktops, laptops, printers, modems, and routers lined up with work orders attached. He had thought he would spend some time researching Prudence Patterson, but it seemed duty called. "Looks like Sussex County went haywire while I was gone."

"This is just the tail end of it. I finished all the backed up work before this pile came in. Have to say it's been pretty busy here," Jared explained.

Vern thought how this rush of business would offset the money he had paid Pru. Marla was still burning about that. She reminded him of how when her brothers had needed money, they didn't give them a penny. But Vern knew she didn't want to and had used him as an excuse as so many couples did when they wanted to wriggle out of a tight spot. In this case, he figured the expenditure was worth it if it would put them closer to finding his birth parents. The papers they had been able to procure from the adoption agency gave him details of the adoption and his parents but no names. Nor would they divulge the names. He was uncertain of where he was born, so that avenue was pretty obstructed. Which state could he apply to? And what name would he use? So, all in all, he was not unhappy to part with the cash, especially since he had almost had to force it on Pru when her guilty feelings surfaced and she tried to refuse it. He had told her she could consider it a loan if she wanted and pay it back when times were better for her. His greater concern was whether or not Pru's mother would actually help him. He hoped she would call him that evening while he was with Marla. He sorted through the pile of work orders and plunged into the tasks at hand.

*****

Marla went into the teachers' lounge and right to the fridge. "I'm starving," she said to no one in particular.

"We've missed you," said Kevin, the PE teacher. "I was just saying the other day that I wondered if you were finding time away from the slots to eat."

She laughed as she popped her lean cuisine into the microwave and punched the time. "Never missed a meal," she joked.

Sybil crashed through the door in her usual manner. "Hey, Kramer," said Ben, "you're just in time to welcome back our high roller!" Kevin was famous for giving out nicknames to the staff, and the grand entrances Sybil made were suggestive of the Seinfeld character.

Sybil took her yogurt container from the fridge and sat at the table next to Marla's place. When Marla brought the steaming meal to the table and sat down, Sybil asked quietly, "And did our Sir Marmalade tell you how royally I treated him?"

"Yeah, he practically ignored me, sniffing around like I was some stranger. I feel a little jealous."

"If you ever get tired of him, I have first dibs. Seriously, how did your trip go?"

Marla looked around the table and saw that Kevin was waiting for a rundown, too. He seemed to sense Marla's hesitancy and put his hands up in surrender and said, "This looks like a Girls' Night Out chat coming up."

Marla laughed and said, "It might not be lunch table conversation, so I'll save all the juicy parts for after school." Looking at Sybil, she said, "Come on over later and we'll have our girl to girl talk." Looking back at Kevin and two others who had joined the table, she recounted her description of the casino, the Strip, the flight with emphasis on the slots at McCarran Airport, and the dinners she had enjoyed. The only staff member who knew the real reason for the trip was Sybil.

Marla did not mention Pru in her recap of events. She still felt a little ill at ease discussing the adoption, had been embarrassed about revealing Katherine's confession. She felt that was Vern's issue to reveal, not hers. Several people had seen the Facebook posting and asked what that was about. Marla had told them that Vern had recently discovered he had cousins somewhere. Everyone knew about her trip to Florida and Vern's mother's illness, but she wondered why she was reluctant to talk about the adoption. Usually she talked about anything and everything at the lunch table but she didn't want to share this.

Sybil arrived at Marla's condo shortly after school let out. She used her key as Marla had instructed and went up the steps, met by Marmalade as she neared the top. He rubbed himself against her and lay on the floor, his snow-white belly up, arching his back and pawing the air. Marla came from the bedroom and witnessed the scene. "Damn!" she said. "He ran into the closet when *I* came home."

"He'll get over it," Sybil told her. She adjusted her flowing neck scarf, picking cat hairs off as she made her way into the dining area. "OK, I smell the coffee brewing. Let's get to the juicy part of your trip!"

They sat at the dining room table and Marla showed Sybil pictures of the buxom Pru at work in the casino, Pru and Vern together outside her car, and half a dozen other shots. "This is one she knew I was taking." She scrolled through the photos on her phone and showed Sybil the close-up of Pru's heart-shaped left earlobe. "This is what did it for them – the proof positive of their relationship."

She told Sybil of the demand for money and Vern's handling of the situation. "You know - I really don't get it how he was so quick to offer to pay her. Of course, she refused the money after Vern calmed her down, but somehow she's got her hooks into him. He actually feels sorry for her. I wanted to rip her eyes out, the bitch." Marla was not famous for profanity but was known to use it from time to time for effect. It sounded comic when she did it because it was always punctuated with a screwed up face and a pout. She saw the smile dancing in Sybil's eyes and went on, "No, really, she is a conniver and I still don't like her."

"You didn't like her before you met her."

"True, and I still don't, probably never will. What I don't understand is Vern's obsession with following through on this. Here's his mother dying of cancer and he's using his energy and time off work looking for a woman who gave him up. She didn't sound like a very nice person, to boot, from the brief references made by Pru the Pill. If that's not the pot calling the kettle black I don't know what is," she mused. She recounted the remark about the drama associated with Grace and the questionable man with the Volkswagen Rabbit and stories of Grace leaving Vern with her mother and the grandmother while she went "whoring," as Pru put it.

"That must've made Vern real eager to meet her," Sybil said.

"Pru's mother is supposed to contact Vern. I think he wants to make his mother more likeable. He said he couldn't take much stock in Pru's assessment, but I think he's in denial. It's like all the years I tried to give my father decent traits he just plain didn't and still doesn't have. My father is a deadbeat, low-life and so are my brothers. It took me a long time to accept that. I think Vern is in the beginning stages of disbelief." She took on her pensive look and tapped the saucer with her spoon. "I also think he thinks he was a very cantankerous child, like somehow it was his fault she gave him up."

"Boy. You'd never think it. If there was ever a Mister Cool, calm-under-pressure guy, it's Vern. On the outside, he looks unflappable, the kind of guy you want around in a crisis." Sybil fixed her gaze on the marsh across the street. "He's as calm as the water is out there today."

Marla looked at the flat, slack-tide water, took a forkful of Entenmann's chocolate cake and savored it. "Well, last night you'd have been reminded of the Nor'easters that blow the whitecaps up on the Bay out there." She recalled Vern's tossing and turning. "He couldn't sleep because he was so anxious about talking to his aunt. Really. Poor guy. There was nothing I could do for him. I'm more anxious about his mother in Florida. She's scheduled to have the tumor removed next week. She arranged it during our Spring Break so I didn't have to take more time off. He'll really be in a bind if Pru's mother wants him to visit his birth mother at the same time as Katherine's surgery."

"Which do you think he'll do?"

"No doubt we'll be heading for Florida but he'll be so distracted. I just want to hug him and sit on a rocking chair with him."

A mischievous look sprang onto Sybil's face. She looked up over her coffee cup and said, "He'd probably be more comforted if you'd throw him on the bed and fuck his brains out!"

Marla burst into laughter. "You really know how to put things into perspective." Recovering, she went on, "Really - he's become such a little boy about this. Seeing those pictures of him living with Pru's family and finding this cousin have made him - I don't know – vulnerable, I guess. When he first found out about his mother's condition, that's when I first saw a needy Vern, one that I can't say I've ever seen in the nearly twenty years I've known him."

"Are you ever going to mention this at school, this newfound family?" Sybil leaned over to pet Marmalade, who was rubbing against her and reaching to be picked up.

"You've stolen my kitty from me," Marla said. "He'll never forgive me for leaving him. When we head back to Florida for Katherine's surgery, that'll really be the final straw for Marmalade!" She watched as Sybil picked her kitten up and snuggled him against her chest. In a more serious tone, she said, "I guess I'll have to say something sooner or later at school about the adoption. I understand why Vern's parents couldn't tell him when they'd missed so many opportunities. It would have been easier for them if they'd told him right from the beginning just like it would have been easier for me if I'd said something at the start of this whole saga."

"You kinda remind me of me and my gay brother," said Sybil.

Marla's eyebrows dipped so far, her eyes nearly closed. "And how is that?" she asked.

Sybil nearly knocked her coffee cup off its saucer as she laughed at Marla's expression. "Let me explain. I have nothing against gays, believe me - but when I first found out about him, I was embarrassed, wondered if it might have been an inherited trait." She stroked her shoulder length hair. "See this long hair? Well, I was always a tomboy and kept my hair short until my brother came out…

"In the beginning I thought people would think I was gay, too. Of course I'm still unmarried, so maybe they do think that. Later, I realized it made no difference, really, whether people thought I was gay or not. I dropped my judgment because that was what I was doing – judging the gay community as one to be embarrassed about. Finally I realized I had no business being embarrassed or making it a topic of conversation. I don't talk about my heterosexual sister, so why should I talk about my homosexual brother in terms of what they do behind closed doors?" Marmalade started squirming, so she put him on the floor. "Naturally, this is nothing like your situation – except - you seem to be embarrassed or ashamed of the whole affair. People were wondering why you and Vern took off to Vegas with no advance notice, especially after you'd just been to Florida such a short time ago. And then there's the

Facebook posting. It's piquing some interest. And somewhere up there is a cloud of shame, embarrassment, cover-up, or something. You can't keep ignoring this; it's so not you."

"You're right, of course. I wish I had said something when they asked about the Facebook thing. For such a large staff, there's a tiny grapevine and I'm sure it's abuzz. I'll let tidbits out in the lunch room."

"You might be surprised at the staff's reaction. Who knows who else is adopted?"

"But when did they find out - if there *is* a they."

"What difference does that make? Neither you nor Vern elected to keep it a secret; it was his parents. And that's really nobody's business."

Marla poured another cup of coffee and brought the pot to the table, offering it to Sybil. "Neither is this whole mess," she said.

"There's where we differ slightly. You'll be missing time from school for Vern's mother and who-knows-what with this goofy family you've inherited. Then it does become everybody's business, like it or not."

She pursed her lips and raised her eyebrows. " Marla, I've known you too long and know you can't hold this all in on a day-to-day basis. You can't say bugger off to the staff." Sybil liked to use some of the British terms she'd learned from her mother. "Remember the trap you said Vern's parents tangled themselves in by keeping the adoption a secret for so long? Well, I don't want to see you dodging everyone or clamming up in the faculty lounge." She stirred her coffee so hard it sloshed out of the cup. "I can pave the way with those bloody little bits and pieces, those tidbits you were talking about, as we eat lunch if you'd like – let it come up gradually. Maybe some of our colleagues will actually have helpful suggestions. If nothing else, I'm sure you'll find their support a big plus. You're going to need it."

"You're right. I'm always such a big mouth about everything. And our faculty is kind of an extended family. Even though this is nobody's business, I'd feel more normal talking about it now and then."

*****

A few nights later eating dinner at *Just Hooked*, Vern said, "Well, it looks like I'll be calling Pru again," as he drained his second Corona. "I wonder why her mother hasn't called."

Marla poked at her seared scallops and brought a bite to her lips. She stopped mid-air, held the morsel, and said, "Vern, it seems like forever to you, but it's really only been a few days." She popped the food into her mouth, watching for his reaction. As he picked up his phone from the table, looking for calls missed, she went on. "Maybe she couldn't reach her mother and maybe her mother hasn't been able to reach *your* mother yet."

Vern returned the phone to its spot next to his dish and called for the waitress. When she came to the table, he ordered a third beer, something he hadn't done since his early drinking days.

Before it arrived, the phone rang. Vern saw an unfamiliar number pop up on the screen. He hoped it was Pru's mother. Anxious, he took a deep breath and answered the call.

"Vern?" the hesitant voice asked.

"Yes."

"Hi. I'm Jane Seaman - your aunt." She hesitated a few seconds, giving him time to realize who it was. "I'm sorry it's taken me so long to call you. I should have called immediately when Pru gave me your number but I wanted to contact your mother first."

Her voice sounded friendly, upbeat. Vern wondered if she was as curious about him as he was about her and his whole family situation. "No problem. It's only been a few days." He looked over at Marla and noted her amused expression. His anxious impatience was replaced by exhilaration at having the contact with this newfound aunt. "Where do we start? I see yours is a Maryland number. You can't be too far from me."

"I'm not, really. I live in Pasadena, just two hours or so away from you."

" And my mother – does she live near you?"

"No, Vern, she actually lives quite a distance from here."

He thought it strange that she didn't say where, but he ignored it for the time being. " Is she well?" He had so many questions, so much he wanted to know; thoughts came tumbling out in rapid succession.

"She is well. Have I interrupted anything?" asked his aunt. The background noise in the restaurant was loud, making it difficult to hear.

He explained where he was. He walked outside to the front pavement. "Is this better?"

"It's a better connection, but the news I have for you may not be best received standing outside a restaurant."

His heart sank. Didn't she just say his birth mother was well? Was she really dead, sick, in serious trouble of some sort and she didn't know how to tell him? Wouldn't he get to meet her? He looked for a place to sit but finding none, rested a hip and shoulder against a pillar at the entrance.

"Vern, I – I don't know how to tell you this, so I'll just tell you. When I heard about you, I was overjoyed." She seemed to struggle to get her words out. "I remember having you with me when you were just a little guy. Boy, how I loved you and hated to have you out of my life."

Vern sensed that the hesitancy showing in her shaking voice did not bode well. "And?" he said.

"But your mother is not typical. She's always been a keeper of secrets and a very hard-headed woman."

"So maybe she's not ready just now to see me? Is that what you're trying to say?"

"It's more than that. She was not happy to hear that you wanted to see her."

Vern moved from the pillar and leaned against the plate glass window. He put his hand to his forehead. Marla came out when she saw him stroking his eyebrows, pinching them together as if to massage a headache. He shook his head back and forth slowly as she watched him, waiting for his end of the conversation to resume. "Will she talk to me if I call her?" The fact that she was not happy about it hadn't closed the door as far as he was concerned. Vern waited for her to continue, was almost afraid the connection had been broken.

Finally she resumed, "She doesn't want to have *any* contact with you." There was silence as his aunt waited for this news to sink in.

He hoped for some misinterpretation on the aunt's part and asked tentatively, "What did she say, exactly?"

His aunt told him she was angry that he was trying to reach her. She did not want him in her life in any way.

Vern massaged his temples again and looked as though he needed to sit down. He was afraid to ask the next question. "And my father, what about him? Is that who she's married to now?" He thought his birth father was completely out of the picture, but this was the straw he grasped for now.

There was a moment of strained silence until she finally delivered the next blow. "Bad news again, Vern. There's been speculation over the years, but your mother never told anyone who your father is, so I can't help you there."

Another dead end. He looked at Marla so pitifully she wanted to take him in her arms right in front of the restaurant.

They continued the discussion with an invitation to Vern and Marla to come to his aunt's house for a family get-together that summer. They would stay in touch and she would work on his mother to try to get her to come. She told him of the three grown children his mother, Grace, had, two of whom lived in the general area. "But I have to caution you – "

"What is it?" He interrupted her as she hesitated, his body tense. He silently prayed that they were well and would like to meet him.

"They don't know about you."

"What?" He couldn't believe what he heard.

"They don't know you exist."

This information was like a stab in the heart. "Didn't she ever tell her family? You knew about me; didn't you ever tell them?"

"My sister told me if I tell her husband and kids about you, she will never speak to me again. Actually, she warned me about that years ago, when the first one, your half-brother Joe, was born." Her painful hesitation surfaced again. "And she brought it up again in our conversation yesterday."

"Why? Why did she have to hide me?"

"My sister has her own demons, Vern. Why does anybody do the strange things they do?"

"And her husband? When they were dating? Didn't he know about me?" Vern thought about how he and Marla shared everything. She'd revealed from the beginning her family matters. He told her about previous girlfriends, about almost being thrown out of school for drinking in the dorms, about forging IDs for himself and friends so they could get beer, and the worst – the DUI he'd gotten the summer they met. Everything that needed to be aired out was done in the course of their dating. They had no secrets. He couldn't believe Grace would hide such a thing as a child. Him....

"My sister is a strange duck, Vern. I guess I shouldn't speak. I have my own quirks."

"Would you have hidden this from your husband?"

113

"If you were mine – no. Nor would I have given you up."

"But Pru remembers that I lived with you. Has she never said anything to her cousins?"

"Well, here's another thing that's hard to tell. Vern, I'm so sorry we're having this conversation on the phone. I'd rather tell you these things in person."

He could hear her voice choke. Then she continued. "She told me to tell them you died when, in fact, you left my home to be adopted."

He flinched visibly, the strength of it seeming to cast a tremor through Marla. He saw her react but recoiled, turning from her. He regained his composure and looked apologetically at her. "And your husband? He went along with this, too? The grandparents? They did, too?"

"I'm sorry to have gone along with it, but it was easier. It wasn't that hard to do because when they first asked, they wanted to know when you were coming back, and I just told them what I had before when you'd leave – that I didn't know."

"And that was the end of it? Of me?"

" After a while they didn't ask anymore. They were so young, too." She repeated, "They never asked. And Grace's husband and kids have never known of your existence."

They both were silent, he – lost in the suddenness and strangeness of it all, she – in the effort and anxiety the telling had exacted on her. The aunt was the first to pick up the tangled strand. "Grace was in and out of all our lives. She'd take you to my parents' farm in Wisconsin and leave you there while she was roaming the country, picking up jobs as a waitress here and there. When she left you with me and I arranged the adoption, she swore me to secrecy."

"This is too weird," Vern said. He stuck his finger in his ear to muffle the sound of motorcycles racing down Coastal Highway. He had her repeat the last part of her sentence, which had been lost in the rumbling.

"My husband thought you'd just moved on. I'm ashamed that I went along with her."

"How was my *death* explained?" He looked over at Marla and saw her wide-eyed stare and horrified look.

"Like I said, we didn't see her or even hear from her for long stretches. I think there were others who cared for you, too – besides me and my parents. When she told me to adopt you out, she told me she was going to spring the death story when people started to ask about you."

"So I guess your husband didn't know about the adoption either."

"Yet another thing I hate to admit. I'm really part and parcel of this whole cover-up. He just came home one day and saw that you were gone and asked if the gypsy had picked you up. It was easier to just say yes and put supper on the table."

Vern tried to imagine Marla in Jane's place. Or himself in his uncle's place. It was so bizarre he couldn't put himself or Marla in their shoes.

She continued, "He accepted it as business as usual and about six months later, we got the news from Grace that you had been hit by a car. Dead and buried in Ohio somewhere. End of story."

Vern could hear the guilt and sorrow in Jane's voice. Nothing could change the history of the events. He figured she had suffered enough revealing it and was grateful that she was not rejecting him like his birth mother was. Another cadre of motorcycles was making its way south to Ocean City. They were near the Fenwick Island information center but Vern could already hear them loud and clear. "Well, Aunt Jane, it's going to be pretty noisy out here for a while, so how about if we talk again?" Vern said.

He could hear and almost feel her relief as she told him how she looked forward to meeting him and was so glad to be part of his life again.

Vern and Marla went back into the restaurant to finish their now cold dinner. The third Corona was sitting there. He sucked on the lime and grimaced, "Perfect tidbit for that news. What do you make of all this?"

"When did the term *dysfunctional family* become popular?" she asked. "I first heard it when I was in college and realized that was a good description of my family. In fact, I thought of your family as one of the few *functional* families I knew." She scraped some of his orzo mac and cheese onto her plate. "Now it seems we have another thing in common!"

"What? The crazies or same taste in food?" He pushed his half-eaten dinner toward her. "Enjoy yourself. I've suddenly lost any appetite."

The waitress stopped at their table and offered to heat their food. While they waited for the plates to come back, Marla reached for his hand and said, "Vern, we can get through this together. Really, you never knew about them and your life was fine. Our life was fine. Can you re-capture that feeling and go on without chasing after them? They don't deserve you." Her eyes teared as she slid her hand back.

"You know how you always say you can't unscramble the eggs? Those half-siblings carry a half egg same as mine. Knowing about them makes it even more important to me. I want to meet them, at least see them."

"I'll bet they'd want to see you just as much. This is all so unbelievable."

Marla's concern snapped Vern out of his self-absorption. He smiled as he said, "If nothing else, maybe we can get to know my aunt and cousins and see if they're all loony." He downed some more of his beer. In a more melancholy tone, he continued, "I still want to see her, too – Grace – see what kind of a woman can just turn her back on her child. I wonder if she ever even thought of me all these years." He clenched his jaw and shook his head as though shaking the thoughts away. The pain in his eyes did not go unnoticed by his wife.

*****

At home, Vern called his parents to see how the arrangements were going for the surgery. His father told him that his mother was prepared for whatever happened and was eager to see them. His father asked how the search was going. When Vern told him the news that his Aunt Jane had given him, his dad said, "I'm not surprised. From what Jenny said, she was a strange one.

And from what you said about Pru, she's a bit strange, too!" James Alexander was silent for a moment.

Vern could hear his mother calling in the background, "Is that Vern? Let me talk to him."

"Hi, beautiful," he said to her. "Do you have your latest fashion in hospital wear packed?"

"Gettin' there," she replied.

"Marla's already putting together our bags. In just a week we'll be down there." He recounted what he had told his father about his aunt's conversation, and she, too, assured him that his birth mother was a bit of an anomaly.

"In her defense, I can only say that if she has led her life ignoring your existence, it might be impossible for her to come clean now." She paused, as though she were looking for the right words to follow that seeming defense of Grace. Vern's tone had implied a dislike, distaste, and growing resentment of his birth mother. Katherine Alexander knew that this resentment could only hurt her son and she wanted to modify it. "Don't forget - she has three grown children, who possibly think she's the perfect mother – to them, anyway. It may upset her to bring you out now."

Vern dimpled as he thought how Katherine always said there were three sides to a story – his, hers, and the truth. He knew she was trying to understand Grace's truth.

"Think of how reluctant I was with *our* secret. You'd be a lot tougher to explain after all these years. In *my* pathetic defense, it was kind of a sign of the times that people didn't always inform their children they were adopted. It's different now."

"I guess you're right. Incidentally, you don't need a defense." He grinned toward Marla, who was trying to get close enough to hear the conversation. "I'm putting you on speakerphone now before Marla breaks one of my ribs."

Marla gave a thumbs up at his action.

"Back to Grace. Now that I have a name I won't have to call her my birth mother anymore. I don't think I want to attach mother of any kind to her name." His voice betrayed the anger that was surfacing toward this strange woman, that Katherine had already detected. "Don't you think she'd have thought of me from time to time? And what about my half-sisters and a half-brother? I want to meet them."

"Curiosity killed the cat," his mother chided, quietly.

He interrupted quickly, "But satisfaction brought it back."

"In a way, I wish I hadn't told you about the adoption. This must be very painful to you to be rejected again by this woman who – you're right - doesn't deserve to wear the title *mother*, no matter what the reasons are for her not wanting to see you."

Vern pondered the message. "No matter where this leads, I'm glad you told me. And I'll handle it. And by the way, you *do* deserve the mother title." He hesitated a second and playfully added, "Even if you didn't always let me have my way."

In his mind, he could see her jerk her head up and glare into the phone. "Really? And when did our little Prince ever *not* get his way?"

119

Fran Hasson

Chapter 10

Anything that is given can be at once taken. We have to learn never to expect anything, and when it comes it's no more than a gift on loan.
John McGahern, *The Leavetaking*

SHE LAY IN THE WAITING AREA, tensely anticipating the pre-op explanations. James would be allowed into the room when the team arrived to give her the mandatory talk - disclaimers, she imagined – warnings that she could die on the table or later as a result of surgical complications or post-operative infections. They had to cover all bases before taking your life into their hands.

She just wanted it over. Katherine had been feeling better since the stents had been inserted. Her appetite had improved and she was looking healthier than she had in the past year. Too bad I have to have the surgery now, she thought, when I'm feeling so good.

The past few days with Vern and Marla were precious. She had cooked Vern's favorite meals: grilled lamb chops and shrimp scampi; had stuffed him with banana pancakes, crispy bacon just the way he liked it, and homemade biscuits slathered with the jam she had preserved.

She had always loved mothering Vern. From the first day they brought him home from the social services office, she had doted on him. And still did when she got the chance: fixing his favorite meals, buying socks and T-shirts when she travelled, sending birthday, Easter, Christmas, Halloween, Thanksgiving cards – any occasion where it would be "permissible" to shower love on her only child. She included Marla in her giftgiving, too. It was not just the "politically correct" thing to do. She loved Marla as a daughter. She agreed wholeheartedly with Vern's choice. He'd had many girlfriends. She always approved of his choices, but she knew the minute he brought her home to meet them that Marla was *the one*.

*****

In the past she had not wanted Marla puttering around in the kitchen when she was preparing meals. She wanted to wait on them. But this time she insisted on Marla being there, showed her how to season the shrimp, marinate the lamb, roll out the biscuits. Just in case. Her eyes watered as she considered the *just in case*.

Marla had told her how Vern talked about the monumental differences between his mother and Grace. She told Katherine that he wondered if she doted over the three children she'd borne in this current marriage. Had Grace's experience with Vern made her realize how precious these children were? Or was she just plain callous and cold. "Vern's beginning to wonder if his aloofness over the years comes from Grace. If it's a genetic thing," Marla told her mother-in-law.

Katherine didn't realize how he'd had to fight his tendencies over the years to share his feelings and his fears with his wife. "I remember how I had to pry things out of him when he was a child. I'd always know when something bothered him, but he'd never tell me unless I kept after him." She told her how he didn't tell her when someone had stolen his bike, how he hid his reports that were not A's and B's, how he couldn't eat lunch because kids teased him about the cutesy notes Katherine had included in his lunchbox. "He seemed to have acquired the British stoicism he'd mistakenly believed he'd inherited from his father."

Marla laughed at that. "Yeah, that's exactly what he's said from time to time – that he has James's stiff upper lip." She wiped floury hands onto the apron Katherine had given her. "But now he wonders if it's simply that he's not affected by some of my drama." She rolled her eyes. "And believe me, I've had my share."

"Who hasn't?" agreed Katherine.

"Sometimes I'd practically have to throw a tantrum before he'd realize how serious I was."

Perhaps he had the same temperament as Grace, thought Katherine, the ability to squirrel away facts and feelings into some compartment in his brain where sticky issues didn't bother him, details that would have levelled others. "There might be something to that. That mentality."

Katherine had learned over the years that her daughter-in-law's fierce loyalty and determination drove her; whereas Vern was content to sit back and only dive in when all seemed lost. "I remember when he was a lifeguard in Bethany Beach, how he was able to sit on that high bench, watching, observing. James and I spent more time watching Vern than we did looking for dolphins or people-watching. We noticed how he only acted when it was obvious there was a need. Like he had this uncanny ability to know what was important." She laughed at the thought. "We figured it was an 'efficiency of moves,' a strategy James taught him when they played chess."

"I think this ability – nature or nurture – has served him well," Marla told her mother-in-law. "He's always avoided the highs and lows of many of our friends and colleagues. My friend, Sybil, calls him Mr. Cool."

*****

Katherine laughed at that label Sybil had given Vern as she lay waiting for the medical staff to bombard her with their mandatory information. She wondered if, despite his coolness, Vern now doubted himself. Now that he knew of the detached Grace, would he see his coolness as a positive trait or as an attitude of carelessness - not caring, the way his birth mother didn't care about him? More than ever Katherine knew that Vern needed her in his life. This startled her. Did she mean he needed *her* or that he needed *Grace* in his life?

She remembered someone telling her when her mother died, "You only have one mother." Vern, in reality, had two mothers. She was more afraid for Vern than she was for herself. She was afraid that he would envelope himself in grief if she should die now. It would be the perfect time for Grace to step up to the plate and be a real mother to him. Knowing Vern, though, she knew how he truly felt about her, how no one would take her place. But she hoped he would drop his resentment and allow this woman into his life – if she would come into it.

James entered the room dressed out as the doctors were: surgical mask, scrubs, hairnets, and sterile booties over their shoes. The surgeon explained that they wanted to risk no contamination. One by one the surgeon, anesthesiologist, and physician's assistant informed them of the procedure. They even had a nurse on hand who would "translate" the medical jargon into understandable terms.

"We're using the Whipple procedure," explained the doctor.

A curious grin lit Katherine's eyes. She wanted to ask if they were going to squeeze the Charmin first but knew this was serious business. The translating nurse smiled at Katherine and explained that *this* Whipple had nothing to do with the old TV commercial, that in this case they were going to use a standard procedure for pancreatic surgery. Katherine's amusement vanished as she set her mouth in a tight line to receive the rest of the news about the surgery. First they would examine laparoscopically. They would biopsy the mass but if they did not see more tumors than they had originally seen on the pre-operative CAT scan, they would proceed with removal of the tumor and reconstruction of the stomach and small intestine to allow normal digestion.

"And if you see more, then what?" asked Katherine, her bravado absent.

The surgeon said, "If that's the case, we cut through the abdominal wall and remove any metastasized tissue and surrounding area plus lymph nodes and do a more extensive reconstruction."

She let this scenario sink in and asked, her voice shaking and skin considerably paler, "Do I have to sign any more papers?"

"No," the doctor said. "Your original consent form states that that we may have to remove lymph nodes and other damaged tissue."

Katherine turned her head as each staff member enumerated the dangers: stroke, cardiac arrest, kidney failure, and some others, most striking of which was death. They delivered this list to James as well as to Katherine. He held her hand and stroked her forearm as each complication landed like a blow. He kissed her before they wheeled her into the operating room. "I'll be waiting for you along with Vern and Marla," he said softly.

"Don't worry, I won't run off with Mr. Whipple," she joked bravely as they took her away.

She often hid her fear with humor, a quality that got her through many tough spots. In this case, as she peered up at the lights above the operating table, she imagined them as flies with many-faceted eyes penetrating the depths of her abdominal cavity, seeking out every grain of cancer. She pictured the one they told her was the "Floater nurse" as hovering out of the room to tell James the operation was a success. The anesthesiologist introduced the "Scrub nurse" to her. She pictured her scrubbing all the cancer cells from her body as she looked down at the draped table next to her. Little did she know but under the drape were the scalpels, clamps, and sponges – not the kind she was envisioning.

The plastic-wrapped laparoscopic tools were gift-wrapped presents for her to open at the conclusion of the surgery, and the blue-coated surgical team were guests at her masquerade party, hiding behind their surgical masks. When she spied the monitors that would record everything that went on, she thought of Vern's old first-generation Apples, the ones that launched him into the world of computers. Vern. Always Vern on her mind these days.

These were her thoughts as they began to hook up all the IVs and necessary tubes, which thankfully Katherine did not have to endure because the Valium had calmed her down and put her to sleep quickly. Her very last thought was of chubby little blonde-haired Vern sitting on James's lap, his hand reaching over to grasp hers, at the photographer's studio the week after they brought him home.

Ten hours later, after the more invasive procedure was finished and the anesthesia had worn off, Katherine opened her eyes. Despite the intense pain, she tried to reach for James and Vern, who stood masked behind their paraphernalia in the Intensive Care Unit. Their worried looks were more painful than the incision. "I told you I wouldn't run off," she muttered past the breathing tube.

*****

When the heart monitor graphed like an Alpine chain and buzzers sounded, Vern knew something was going very wrong. Katherine choked for breath, turned blue, and writhed. Then she was still. Nurses came running, calling "Code Blue!" They rushed the two men from the ICU. Vern resisted and they called for help to remove him from the room. "That's my mother! What's happening?" James was paralyzed by fear and just did what he was told. He kept looking back over his shoulder as he was escorted from the room. "Katherine," he whimpered.

Marla waited outside the room. She saw the flurry of activity and tried to peek inside. While the door was open to allow Vern and James out, she could see carts with machinery rolling past, see the masked attendants rushing toward Katherine, could even hear the beeping and banging the defibrillator made.

They spent thirty anxious minutes, pacing and standing close to the door, trying to pick up what was going on. Vern wanted a cigarette. He had never smoked but had tried it during his college years. Not only did he know it was unhealthy, he didn't like it. Now he wanted something to do to ease the stress. He had seen movies where the hero would reach for a cigarette in situations like this and he thought it would calm him. Marla hugged him from time to time, alternating between comforting him and tending to his father. Vern watched James sitting, hunched over in the leather chair, his face in his hands, sobbing.

"That monitor went flat as we were walking out," James said.

Vern hadn't noticed because he was being escorted out, an attendant holding each arm. He had craned back to watch the activity of the technician placing the defibrillator pads on his mother and hadn't looked at the monitor.

The door to the ICU opened and a doctor emerged, pulling his mask off as he approached them. Vern saw the grave look on his face and anticipated the bad news. "I'm so sorry," he murmured, "but we lost her."

The three crushed into each other as one. Both men huddled around Marla, holding her close to them. It was hard to know if they were comforting her or taking comfort from her. Vern spoke first, his voice breaking as he managed the words. "What happened?"

The doctor extended his arm, led them to the chairs in the waiting area, where he beckoned them to be seated. He sat next to James. "As you know, the surgery went longer than expected, which meant we found extensive spread of the cancer. Your wife seems to have thrown a clot." He shook his head sadly and nodded toward the ICU. "We did everything we could in there to pull her out of it, but it was either a massive stroke or heart attack and there was nothing more we could do."

Vern felt his world crumble. "I told you I wouldn't run off" – Those words echoed in Vern's mind then and for years after. They were the last words he ever heard his mother say.

He wanted to talk to her again, to tell her what a great mother she was, that he knew she wouldn't run off like Grace had. He wanted to invite her to Fenwick Island where they could sit on the beach, take her on a fishing boat where she would watch him and James try their luck. She always enjoyed the ride, looked for dolphins, saved up the best "fish tales" for Marla, who would be at work while they went out on their expeditions. He wanted to feel her cheek against his, see her famous smile. He bowed his head and tried to hide his tears. Marla slid closer to him, keeping an eye on both men.

James was alone with his grief. Marla went over to him and sat next to him, put both her arms around him. He stared down at his hands, and when he looked up, his gaze was distant and empty. He had no words. Marla knew Katherine would expect her to be strong. "Women are definitely the stronger species," she had told Marla on many occasions. Now the younger woman had to be the one to support these two devastated men.

The next days were a blur. At first they were in shock, unable to grasp the fact that she was gone. Vern and Marla consoled James and each other as best they could. When the realization sank in and they had to make arrangements for the funeral, notification of others, and the burial, Vern busied himself. He looked at all the old photographs, compiling a CD for the funeral service. Nearly all the pictures in the albums had him in them. He found some of James' and Katherine's wedding, and some other "pre-Vern" pictures of his parents at the beach, Katherine on the back of a motorcycle holding onto James, the two of them dressed as jester and queen. "I don't remember this motorcycle," said Vern.

James chuckled. "Your mother made me sell it when we got you," he said. "Too dangerous for our little prince."

Vern managed a sad simper. "I really was the center of her universe." Remembering their conversation from his visit before and James's reaction, he quickly added, "And yours, too."

*****

Vern and Marla left James with a sad and heavy heart. He refused to come with them, saying he'd manage. They knew how difficult that would be, the two having spent forty-five years together, but they went back to Delaware with the promise that they would call him every day.

On the plane Vern said, "I guess I should call my aunt and tell her the news. Right now I really don't want to see Grace, so she can tell her to relax." It seemed to him that she would be glad to know he was dropping his search for her.

They both returned to work, settling back into their routines with the added feature of speaking to James every day. Vern could hear the sadness in his father's voice, the hollowness echoing through the lines, mirrored by the imagined loneliness of their home, the cross-stitch pieces reminding him daily of the missing Katherine. He told them how he'd go to Dagwood's and the Scampi Grill for the early bird specials two or three times a week and fix meager meals for himself the rest of the time, sometimes not eating at all for a day or two.

Vern said, "There are days when you don't eat anything?"

"I'm just not hungry."

"Dad, why don't you come up here with us just for a few weeks?"

"It might not be a bad idea. I keep seeing your mom everywhere around here. I guess the reminders should be a comfort...." His voice broke. "But it makes me miss her even more."

"I can imagine," said Vern. "But if you come here just for a while, it might be a good transition for you."

And so it was that James came to live with them for a short time. He took up residence in the guest room and enjoyed watching the activity on the Bay from his room, the same room where Marla's mother had spent her last days. James was a handyman at heart. He went right to work repairing the screen doors, installing handrails on their entrance steps, and tending to Marla's garden. At night when they sat on the back deck, Vern could see James's eyes misting over as he listened to the fountains gurgling on the lagoon. And when he returned from walking on the beach, Vern noticed how his body sagged. At such times, he wanted to ask him if he was thinking about Katherine, but he knew he was and was afraid to bring the subject up. He was afraid his father might cry, that he wouldn't know how to comfort him. As close as they were, the thought that he was becoming the father and James the son was unsettling.

He realized that Marla was so much better at this than he. She encouraged James to talk about his wife. Hearing stories about her mother-in-law, especially when they were about her and Vern or Katherine and herself delighted her. James's reliving these stories didn't reduce him to tears; on the contrary, Vern watched his father glow as he retold the stories. He thought perhaps the reason he didn't bring it up to his father was that *he* might cry. Glowing with pride at his wife's soothing manner, he listened as she told James about how she treasured the last days when Katherine divulged her recipes.

"A testament to how much she thought of you," said James. "She never gave anybody those secrets."

"More a testament to Vern. I know she did it because she wanted me to carry on her traditions." Marla was rolling out biscuits for chicken and dumplings. "She told me she had a box of recipes. Do you know where she kept them?"

"Sure do." James smiled as he watched Marla's floured hands cutting the biscuits with the edge of a drinking glass. "You even use the same cutters as she did."

"Yeah, she told me this was the best method."

"Next time I come up or when you come down, the secret recipe box is yours."

Fran Hasson

Chapter 11

Experiment to me
Is everyone I meet
Emily Dickinson, *Experiiment*

JAMES WAS STILL STAYING WITH VERN AND Marla when they went to the cook-out at Jane's house. Although they had offered to take him along, he stayed home with Marmalade. "Maybe next time," he said. "This first meeting shouldn't be awkward." He smiled, a whimsical look showing. "If your mother were here, it would be better. Nothing was awkward when she was around."

"I'm sure they'd welcome you just as they will us," said Vern. "But there will be a next time, and we'll drag you along as a captive."

Marla gave Marmalade a last hug, handing him over to James. "He's been seeing more of you than he has me. He likes you." The kitten rolled over in James's arms, settling into his chest.

*****

They drove past middle class neighborhoods where all the homes were of the same model, differing only in color, yard décor, and variety of mid-range vehicles parked along the street. Strip malls were everywhere, highways were congested, and traffic heading to BWI airport signified, along with Tom-Tom's mileage counter, that they were nearing their destination. As they got closer to the Chesapeake Bay, the difference in home quality loomed large. Palatial estates sat back from the road, long tree-lined driveways approaching the entrances and circling back to the highway. Lawns were professionally landscaped with topiary designs, hedgerows, large towering trees, and copious varieties of flowering plants.

"Too bad we weren't here before Memorial Day," said Marla. "I'd love to have seen those magnolia blooms at the height of the season. I suppose there were plenty of tulips and daffodils, too," she said as she pointed out the remaining leaves.

Scattered among the mansions were one and two-storey homes made tiny in comparison. These homes also featured manicured lawns with less ostentatious displays. "That's the kind of place we'd live in," said Vern.

"I don't think so," replied Marla. "I'll bet these people bought their places years ago before the Chesapeake became so desirable. Their neighbors are probably waiting for them to die off so they can buy them and tear them down."

Tom-Tom led them to Jane's house before noon. The parking space directly in front of Jane Seaman's house was open, a sign tacked onto a board saying, *Reserved for Vern and Marla Alexander.* Vern parked the car. Gathering the wine and bouquet, they made their way up the steps to the paved walkway.

"Looks like a red carpet welcome," said Vern.

"I'm nervous," said Marla. "I wonder if Pru will be here." She remembered the visit to Pru's home and how they had gotten off on the wrong foot. She didn't want to repeat that. Vern had been looking forward to meeting these cousins. If they were like their sister, she was afraid the day would be a calamity. Worse, that she might open her big mouth with some unintended insult.

"Probably not." Vern reassured her. They had discussed earlier that they expected the other three cousins - Carlie, Shelly, and Jack. "It's strange, isn't it – having this whole slew of cousins with families?"

"I forget. Are we the only ones with no kids?"

"It's hard to keep up with all these new relatives. I think Shelly's not married and the other two each have two kids." He admired the entrance to Jane's house. "I already have the feeling my mother would have liked Jane," he said as he passed the multi-colored gladiolas that lined the walk. Her flowerboxes hanging from the windows boasted bright red geraniums set off by brilliant orange marigolds and deep purple petunias. His mother had been gone nearly three months, but feeling the warmth generated by Jane's home brought her presence to the moment. The smell of the charcoal coming from the backyard reminded him of the cook-outs his mother always raved about in their Vero Beach community, causing him to ache at the memory and desire to have the two meet.

The closer they got to the front door, the louder was the chatter from within and from the backyard. Young children's voices pierced the air, the laughter bringing smiles to their faces. "Sounds like a faculty picnic," said Marla.

"Maybe even like a family picnic," said Vern. "Something we've never heard before."

A teenager came to the door. Her broad grin and warm welcome banished Marla's nervousness, and Marla returned the smile with one broader than the girl's. "You must be the mystery cousins everybody's talking about," the girl said. "I'm Maribel. Come on in and don't be afraid if everybody comes at you at once."

Vern followed Marla into the living room where a crowd, having heard the doorbell, gathered. Aunt Jane led the charge. "Vern." The simple greeting was followed by arms outstretched, the hug that followed nearly suffocating him. "And Marla." She gathered her as she gave a bear hug to both.

As introductions were made and the two were led through the kitchen, given drinks, and fawned over, Vern was overwhelmed. "Do you feel like royalty?" he whispered to Marla.

"I guess. We should have practiced the *wave*," she said.

His cousin, Jack, pulled Vern aside. "It's great to have another man in the house. Ed and I have been doing all the barbecueing the past few years." He told him how his father had been killed in a car accident five years earlier. "It's pretty scary. My uncles, they died before I was born, died the same way." He dragged Vern away, leaving Marla in the center of her new family.

"I'm not such a great cook," admitted Vern. "We live in an upstairs condo and aren't allowed grills on the deck."

"Not to worry. Come meet Ed, Sally's husband. He's been tending the fire while everyone else bombarded you and Marla."

Vern looked back at Marla as though asking permission to leave her there in the middle of the other women and the already adoring thirteen-year-old Maribel. When the girl found out that Marla's mother's maiden name was the same as hers, that cemented her. She was now more like a big sister than second cousin by marriage, and Maribel clung to her throughout the day.

Jane took Vern aside, leaving the brothers-in-law to do the grilling. She led him to the gazebo facing the Chesapeake Bay. They watched the boaters enjoying the afternoon sun, colorful spinnakers and mainsails skimming the water, pushed on by the light breeze. Jane kept an eye on Jack's two young sons, who came too close to the entrance to the dock from time to time. "Maribel won't let Marla out of her sight," Jane said. " She's keeping her eye on her like I am on these boys." She reached over and touched his knee. "I'm so happy to have you with us."

"Same here," he said. "But Grace doesn't share your joy."

She saw the concern wash over his face. "I'm hoping someday she'll come around. When I told her about your mother, I thought maybe that would spark some feeling in her, that she'd want to reach out while she still has time."

"I'm not even sure I still want to meet her," admitted Vern. This surprised Jane. He saw the question form on her face and continued. "I'm still curious but when my mother died, I wondered why I was trying to find this woman who never wanted me. I decided to just meet you and your family and then take it from there."

"My sister is a strange one," said Jane. "There are just the two of us. I've kept her secrets over the years without question. I'm kinda like one of her dogs, just adoring her purely because she's my sister, my only sibling. I've been giving her the unconditional love she always talks about."

"Who's older?"

"I am. I guess that's another factor – I feel like I have to protect her."

Jack's three and four year-old sons sneaked up on the two in the gazebo. Vern saw them coming but pretended he didn't. They both jumped into the enclosure at once. The older one, Ben, buried himself in Jane's lap while Grant stuck his index finger in his mouth and cautiously examined Vern.

"I'm so thankful that you have welcomed me into this brood." He motioned to the towhead. "Come here. What's your name?"

The youngster sidled over to his grandmother, keeping a watchful eye on Vern and sucking harder on his finger.

"He's Grant and I'm Ben," the older brother offered happily. "He's shy."

"And you're not," Jane said, tousling his hair and bouncing him on her knee.

So this is what it's like to have a family, thought Vern. He realized this was the first time he'd had a pure happy moment since Katherine Alexander had died. "Thank you so much , Jane, Aunt Jane." It felt awkward to use the family name. "What should I call you?"

"Grace's other children call me Aunt Jane."

"Somehow I don't feel like Grace's child."

"You are, though. But I really don't mind what you call me just so you call me and don't make this your last visit."

The day was full of food, fun, and family. Vern totally enjoyed meeting his cousins and his aunt. The high point of the day was when little Grant rushed him like a linebacker and held onto his leg. "Piggy," he implored.

When Vern looked toward Jack, he told him, "You're in. He wants a piggyback ride."

He readily adapted to the role of both cousin and chef with Ed and Jack instructing him on when to turn the chicken, when to slather the ribs, and how to test the hamburgers for rare and well-done. He told Marla, "Don't get any big ideas. You're still head chef."

They sat around the square wooden picnic tables, Maribel leaving Marla only long enough to bring out pitchers of iced tea and bowls of Jane's family recipe potato salad. Vern sat across from Marla with his little pal waiting to be served. Grant wanted to eat what Vern wanted to eat. Vern and Marla exchanged glances. It was obvious Vern fit right in with the family and so did Marla.

After eating, Jane led the two into the living room. She shooed Maribel away with instructions to help with clean-up. "I thought you might like to see some family photos, especially of when you lived with us."

The living room reflected the family. Pictures on the wall of her parents' farm in Wisconsin, Jane's family portraits taken over the years, Grace with her husband and children, family pets – every wall was covered with these photos, some yellowed with age. Fischer-Price toys were scattered about, children's books were on the coffee table and bookshelf, and a pile of knitting yarn, needles, and unfinished pieces sat in a basket in the corner of the room.

"How about if we start at the wall?" suggested Vern. He moved to the yellowed farm photo. There was a wooden shingle hanging from the front porch under which stood an elderly couple.

"My parents," said Jane.

The sign on the porch read *Bjork Bastion*. "What does that mean?" he asked.

"My dad always said his home was his castle, and he thought Bjork Bastion sounded fancier than Bjork Castle."

Vern tucked this away. Grace and Jane Bjork. He didn't want to put Jane in the middle. She had told him beforehand she wouldn't give him information that would lead him to Grace, but he saw her discomfort as she swallowed a lump in her throat and moved quickly away from the photo.

However, there was no escaping the picture in front of the Botanical Gardens' carved mahogany sign. Both Vern and Marla snapped to attention as they headed right for the framed photo of two smiling subjects – Grace and George Elsmere. "Who are these two?" asked Vern, a tightness in his voice.

"That's your mother and her husband, George."

"Are they vacationing in this picture?"

"I guess it's safe to tell you that this picture was taken in the Caribbean, where they live. I promised Grace I wouldn't lead you to them and it's a stretch to think you would go there. A greater stretch that you could find them."

Vern drew a deep breath. He did not tell Jane of their contacts and experience on St. Croix five years earlier or that he and Marla were very familiar with the Botanical Gardens and all eighty-four square miles of the island. He decided that if they wanted to look for Grace, he wouldn't tell Jane what a dynamic clue this was.

The two had been on a quest that had led them to St. Croix when Marla had discovered a box of ashes on the beach at Fenwick Island. Her dogged determination to find the owner had led them to the Virgin Islands where a frightening experience had nearly cost Vern his life, but the satisfaction of finding the identity of the person whose ashes Marla had found and the lifelong friends they had made there would forever be etched in their minds.

Seeing this picture renewed his interest in finding Grace. Even though the desire had waned with the death of his mother, the intrigue he associated with that Caribbean island grabbed him. Maybe it was time to visit their old friends, to check up on Darryl, his former boss, who had relocated to St. Croix to be with Rosalie, a woman who had taken them under her wing when they were there on Marla's mission. He looked over at Marla and knew she was reliving that time, too. He knew she was anxious to talk about it and was surely biting her tongue and scrunching her toes against her shoes. They looked at each other but betrayed no emotion that would show Jane how excited they were with this new knowledge.

It was curious, his reaction to seeing the photo. The picture of a younger Grace that he had seen at Pru's had fascinated him in a different way. Before he knew that she didn't want to see him, he had inspected her features, had looked for a longing in that face that wanted to search out her lost son. He had wanted her to be a mother who regretted giving him up, one who would open her arms and run to him. One who would try to make up for the years she had missed. That woman would hold him close, then extend her arms to get a different view of him, would want to know he hadn't suffered as she had all those intervening years.

This Grace showed no signs of having suffered. There she was, all tan and smiling, leaning into her husband, in front of the carved mahogany sign, the iconic sugar mill in the background where so many weddings took place, looking herself like a new bride.

"When was this picture taken?" asked Vern.

"Two years ago. We visited them. I don't want to tell you where in the Caribbean this is, not right now," said Jane. "I'm still working on her."

"It's OK," he said. "I don't want to cause problems between the two of you. If I decide to pursue her, I won't put you in the middle."

Marla moved on to the other wall photos. "Did you say you had pictures of little Vern?" she asked. "I'd like to see if he was just as cute then as he is now." She shrugged and cocked her head like a puppy.

Vern grinned at her comical look, a look he loved. "Yeah, let's see how cute I was," he agreed. They moved to the sofa where Jane had centered two albums on the coffee table. The three-cushioned couch was soft. Marla sank into the floral print while Vern sat straight-backed at the edge, in the middle of the two women. As Jane reached for the top album, Grant toddled in, went right to Vern, and climbed into his lap. Vern beamed and looked at Marla while he hugged Grant close. He was the picture of a doting father. He wondered if Marla was getting any ideas. They had discussed whether or not to have children and had decided against it years ago. Now he wondered if they weren't missing something.

Maybe they should re-visit that decision before their biological clocks wore down. He liked this new idea of family. Having been an only child, he had never known what it was like to roughhouse with a brother, to watch over a sister, to vie for parental attention and compete like the Kennedy clan. He wondered what vacations would have been like sitting in the back seat of a car and pinching a brother, of giggling over things they'd gotten away with, of coming to family picnics and playing with little cousins such as the ones here.

Marla noticed the resemblance between Vern and Grant, made sharper as they looked at photos of Vern when he was about this toddler's age. When the boy turned toward her, she saw the tiny left earlobe with the distinctive heart shape. "Look, Vern, he has your earlobe." Addressing Jane, she said, "Do you or Grace have this feature?"

She was surprised as Jane's face darkened. "No. This is a Seaman trait. My late husband had such an earlobe."

Marla and Vern exchanged wary glances. Uh oh, I think I've touched a nerve, thought Marla. She didn't know what to say next and looked down at the pictures. Was Uncle Bert really Uncle Daddy?

It seemed that Jane had read their minds. "Grace assured me that Bert was not Vern's father. We had this discussion years ago." Her gaze bore into each of them. "Grace may be a lot of things, but she is not a liar. I believe her."

Vern and Marla looked at each other with what must have been a look of disbelief because Jane followed it up with, "We often wondered if she had become involved with one of Bert's brothers because she named you after both of them."

Grant scrambled off Vern's lap and ran to the door. "Wanna go out," he said.

Ben was on the other side of the screen door calling, "Aunt Jane, let me in!"

Maribel rushed to open the door. "C'mon, Ben. I don't know how this got stuck."

The boys ran through the living room to the back door, where they banged the screen door open and shut. Vern and Marla looked at each other. Vern lifted an eyebrow as though the interlude had provided the break they needed from the sticky issue of Uncle Bert.

Marla resumed leafing through the album. "Oh look, Vern," she said, pointing to a picture of Vern, less than two years old, holding a stuffed shark.

"Is that Choss?" asked Vern. "My parents have pictures of me lugging around a little shark like that. They said I called it Choss."

Jane broke into laughter. "One and the same. My mother bought it for you and you couldn't say Jaws. You took that little critter everywhere you went." She flipped through several more pages, pointing out Vern carrying his Choss with one hand, the other hand in his mouth like Grant, the index finger jammed tight between his lips. "Here you are the day you got it. Your grandma snapped a picture of you sleeping with it."

"My mother snapped pictures of me sleeping with it, riding my tricycle with it, feeding it birthday cake and on and on. She said when his dorsal fin fell off and his eyes popped out, she had to cajole me into giving it up." He looked off to the distance. "You know, I still remember crying when she said she was taking him to the shark hospital."

He remembered ending his bedtime prayers with *Please bless Mommy and Daddy and please bring Choss back soon.* "I think I loved that little guy more than anyone besides my parents." He grinned. "Maybe even more."

Vern wanted to tell Aunt Jane about his love of scuba diving and his fascination with sharks. He thought of the aquariums they had visited. Just as Marla had her favorite sections in art museums, Vern could not seem to move away from shark exhibits at aquariums. How many times Marla had moved on to tropical fish, turtles, and other features, leaving Vern gawking at the huge predators in their tanks. He wondered if that fascination had started right there with Grandma Bjork's gift of Choss. He was afraid he might slip and tell her about his shark episode on St. Croix, so he pointed out another picture. "What was the occasion here?"

Aunt Jane told him about Pru's eighth birthday party, the last one he shared with them. All five children sat around the picnic table in the back yard in the same spot where Vern and Marla had sat earlier. "We've gone through a few tables since then and you can see the trees and shrubs have grown quite a bit. Just like you kids."

"I'm curious," said Vern. "None of my cousins have asked me about my mother or the adoption."

"As you can imagine," said Aunt Jane, "I briefed them. They know how weird my sister is and like you, they don't want me to get into trouble with her." She turned to a page where Grace was standing with her parents and Vern. "She has always been Queen of Sheba and we've always bowed down to her." She leaned forward and gave a half-hearted shrug.

"How do you feel about that?" asked Vern.

"It's getting old. I've seen how happy you are and how happy my kids are. Not to mention Grant and

Maribel and the other grandkids." She smiled. "I know her kids would be overjoyed to meet you. But for now I think we have to let her have her way again. Until she decides to open up."

Fran Hasson

Chapter 12

Sir, more than kisses, letters mingle souls;
For, thus friends absent speak.
John Donne, *Letter to Sir Henry Wotton*

"WELL, WHAT DID YOU THINK of our first family picnic?" Vern asked Marla as they pulled away from the house.

"Quite the experience," she said.

"How about Grace living on St. Croix."

"Whoda thunk it?"

"It sure is a small world."

"I'll bet we could find her in no time flat," Marla said. She thought of the picture of Grace and George at the Botanical Gardens. Rosalie would sniff them out in no time, with or without last names. Marla was excited about the thought of returning to St. Croix, of seeing the friends they had made there. She knew the decision was Vern's, though, that this was his mission if he wanted to find Grace. She looked over at him and saw that he was deep in thought as he inflated his upper lip with tightly closed lips. He would blow out puffs of air from time to time or move the air around his lips and cheeks, adopting a tongue-in-cheek look. She always wanted to laugh at the expressions he made in this pensive mood, but she knew it was a sign of stress, that he was mulling thoughts over.

"I'm still not sure I want to pick up the search for her," Vern finally said, after negotiating the traffic and moving into a comfortable line and reasonable speed. They were on Rt. 50 East now and could pretty much stay on automatic pilot the rest of the way home. "I really like this new family. I don't want to do anything to upset Jane's apple cart." He added, "Plus, I'm not sure my dad is ready for a new - mother - to enter my life."

"I understand. And neither are you." She put her hand on his right thigh and let it rest there for a bit.

She thought, too, of James and the resettling process. He was still deep in his grief over the loss of Katherine. Staying at their home gave him the grounding and support he craved. She fixed his favorite foods, washed his clothes in the same detergent Katherine used, even ironed his trousers. She almost never ironed Vern's trousers, merely removed them from the dryer as soon as they finished and smoothed them out to a sharp-enough crease. But James always liked a razor crease in his pants, starched collar and cuffs, and Marla indulged him in these habits. For now.

"Jane said when she told her about my mother, Grace didn't have a response at first. Then the next day she called back and asked if she should send me a condolence card. Jane gave her our address. But we never received anything, did we?"

"You know I'd have given it to you right away if we had." She considered it for a moment and wondered if Grace was afraid of sending something with a St. Croix postmark.

"Maybe she didn't want me to see where it came from," Vern said.

"Took the words right out of my mouth." She thought about how, over the years, they could practically read each other's mind. Their marriage was based on values Vern had gotten from his parents, certainly not hers. Something as simple as not receiving the card would have been the source of suspicion and accusations in Marla's home. Her father would not have hesitated hiding a card from her mother. By the same token, her mother's first reaction to a situation like this would have been to suspect her father of having done something with the card. Vern, in his wildest dreams, would not have thought Marla deliberately would have kept the card from him.

She considered it an honor that James would stay with them during this transition. She was sure there was more that they could learn by his example. Maybe he would consider coming back from Florida and living with them permanently.

"I wonder how Dad's doing with Marmalade. Do you think he's chasing him around with the laser pointer like we do?" Vern asked.

Again, she thought, great minds swimming in the same channel. She replied, "I was just thinking about him – Dad, not Marmalade. Do you think he might want to move in with us? He's never been on his own since he married your mom."

"He might. Let's run it by him. Maybe we can even introduce him to our new cousins and aunt."

"Actually I think he'll like that younger generation, especially Ben and Grant. I think your parents always wanted grandkids."

"Who wouldn't like them?" said Vern. "I have to admit I'm partial to Grant. Wasn't he like a little Cling-on?" He noticed her shocked look. "Not Klingon like a trekkie, but one who clings on, a cling-on."

Marla loved word games. From time to time Vern would come up with some good puns or wordplay, and this qualified. "You're so right. But what did you think about the little cling-on's earlobe and Uncle Bert? I think he's your daddy."

"I wonder if we'll ever know. We should go to St. Croix, kidnap Grace and make her 'fess up." He laughed at this idea. "I once heard someone say you never know for sure who your father is. Judging from my cousins, other than Pru, I'd be OK with Uncle Bert being Uncle Daddy."

"You really seemed to be getting on with Jack."

"It's amazing the coincidences in our lives. We're six months apart in age, he was a lifeguard in Virginia Beach the same years I was at Bethany, we both got our degrees in computer literacy the same year, and we're both married to teachers." He popped a Black Eyed Peas CD into the deck. "Did you get a chance to talk to Mallory? Ha! Another parallel – names that nearly match. In fact, Mallory, Maribel, and Marla!"

Marla lowered the volume to Vern's frown. "What coincidences. Although I know you don't take too much stock in them. But this whole journey into your background reminds me of a line in *Desiderata* that goes *And whether or not it is clear to you, no doubt the universe is unfolding as it should."*

"And your point?" He reached to turn up the CD, but she brushed his hand aside.

"Whether or not you track Grace down, and whether or not Uncle Bert is Uncle Daddy, and even if cousin Pru is a loser, this whole adventure into a new family is right for you. For us."

They rode along in silence, each in his or her own thoughts. They had left Route 50 and were passing endless fields which would be filled with corn and soybeans later in the year. Marla spotted the sign, "Naked Farmer ahead."

What are you laughing about?" Vern asked.

"I find your mom where I least expect her."

"I hope it wasn't the naked farmer sign that announced her arrival." He smiled. "Or maybe it was."

"Actually I remember her saying 'The way I prefer tomatoes, carrots, and potatoes is bare naked'" This was surprising because Katherine Alexander was widely known for her spaghetti sauce – gravy, she called it – a term she had picked up from an Italian friend from South Philly. "I can still see her expression and hear the tone as she said 'bare naked.' She hunched down as though she was telling me a classified secret." She leaned forward in her seat and bent toward Vern. Eyes open as wide as she could, she whispered, "Like this, *bare naked*!"

They continued the drive alternating between lowering and increasing the volume. Whenever Marla wanted to talk, she lowered it. The minute the conversation ended, Vern hiked it back up.

Vern knew he had decisions to make. Pursue Grace or not. Convince his father to move in or not. Invite his new cousins to their home, a few at a time, to be sure, since their condo was so tiny, or not. Would he put them on the spot? He had to clear everything with his Aunt Jane before proceeding with the invitations. He wanted to know what they knew, but he didn't want to invite them to interrogate them. He especially wanted to foster a friendship with Jack and his family.

He was curious about his siblings, too. No one had mentioned them at the picnic, but he knew from Aunt Jane that they had gotten together from time to time. Would the cousins tell Grace's kids about Vern? Had they already? Were they as anxious as he was to meet each other? Or was everyone protecting Grace's secret? If they were, he had to, also. One minute he wanted to open the whole can of worms and spill them out. The next minute he thought how Aunt Jane had really taken a giant leap by divulging this to her kids at such a risk. He knew she loved Grace and couldn't go the extra step and bring Grace's kids into this. And neither would he.

"I'm not so good about keeping secrets like Jane and her kids are," he said to Marla, who seemed to be getting antsy with his long silences. She had dug into her handbag and pulled everything out, piece by piece, reorganized them, and looked in the glove compartment for something to read. Ordinarily they could go for quite a stretch not speaking, but he knew she wanted to discuss this outing and all the points they were touching on. "How long do you think we can go on without meeting my half-brother and sisters? Or at least talking to my cousins about them?"

"For as long as it takes. I think Aunt Jane hit the nail on the head when she said we have to wait until Grace decides to open up." Marla's smile spread across her face as they turned onto Route 54. "Home at last," she said. "Almost, anyway."

Ignoring her joy, he said, "In the meantime I guess we can have a relationship, how funny, a *relationship*, with these few relations." Vern thought about the future get-togethers and how to fold James into the mix. "And my dad – let's try to talk him into moving in. Of course this means a move for us. Would you mind that?"

"Would I mind it? Getting away from that disgusting bar across the street? I think I could live with that. Besides, I still have the occasional nightmare about Sammy and Ophi returning from the dead and bringing their drug deals over there."

Vern thought back to the ordeal they had been through, the St. Croix connection from five years back with the Obeahmen, those wannabe practitioners of voodoo, that Marla was referring to. "But - will you miss the view?"

"That can never be replaced. But a bigger home, a garden, a fenced area where you can have a dog...." She trailed off dreamily and abruptly returned to the main point. "And then there's your dad. Isn't that the main point, having plenty of space for him?"

*****

157

The next time James came to stay with Vern and Marla, it was a permanent move. Vern knew that his dad sorely missed his wife and that women in the neighborhood were giving him the widow's hustle, inviting him for dinners, bringing pies, cakes, and casseroles to the house, encouraging him to come to the community center. But Vern also knew that James was single-minded, and that while he was grateful for their attention, he did not want that level of friendship. Not even the married couples or single men in the community had been able to prod him out of his isolation booth. He had always been devoted to his family and now wanted to be with his son and daughter-in-law.

The only things he brought with him on his next trip were clothes, some picture albums, and the treasure chest, those secret recipes. He hadn't had the heart to go through Katherine's recipes, simply handed the unopened box to Marla when they returned from the airport and he was unpacking his bags.

"I'll go find a quickie recipe for tonight's dinner," she said.

Marla immediately sat at the dining room table and opened the elaborately decorated box. It was a bright red lacquered box covered on all sides with colorful roses, pansies, daffodils, gladiolas, and chrysanthemums – all hand-painted by Katherine. Inside on top of the recipe cards were two sealed envelopes, one addressed to Vern and one to Marla.

She pulled back the shower curtain, startling Vern. "What the hell…" he said.

His protective stance amused her. "I couldn't wait till you got out," she said quietly. "Your dad is in his room unpacking and resting. Look at this." She held his envelope up.

He quickly came out of the shower and wrapped a towel around himself.

"She wrote one to me, too. I haven't opened it yet." She showed him the one addressed to her.

She noticed the care he gave the envelope. He dried himself thoroughly to avoid smearing the writing and worked it open with a pair of scissors from the vanity, almost as if he were afraid to hurt his mother. They sat at the edge of the bed, each handling their letter with delicacy, each absorbed in the communication from beyond.

Hers was a short note, written in Katherine's elegant script. People used to ask her if she had gone to Catholic School, her handwriting so fluid and neat. The words flowed like poetry and touched her heart.

My dear Marla,

You're the daughter we never had. I knew from the beginning that you were the perfect match for my beloved son. Please watch over him and my husband. Encourage him to forgive his birth mother if he should find her. She must have had her demons. And please encourage James to re-marry if he finds anyone as nutty as I have been. I love you and my two boys and if there's a way to watch over you, know that I'll be there.

Katherine

Vern rose and went to his computer which had been moved from the guest room to their bedroom to accommodate James. He sat, transfixed. He wasn't ready to share this with Marla. He needed a moment alone with his mother. When he looked over at her, sitting alone at the edge of the bed, he felt guilty shutting her out. But she nodded at him with the slightest of smiles and re-read her own card.

Even though he'd opened the envelope, he couldn't bring himself to remove the handwritten card. He could see it was a notecard Marla had given her as a gift from the National Gallery, one that Katherine had selected from that box of Impressionist cards. It was *The Boating Party* depicting a man, woman, and child. After caressing the envelope and fingering the card, he gently removed it.

My dear Vern,

If I didn't make it through the surgery, I'm sorry. I'm sorry to leave you and your dad so soon. I know you have a tower of strength in your dear Marla. Lean on her if you need to.

If you continue your search for Grace, please don't compare her to me. Marla told me some of the things you said. It is Grace's loss that she has excluded you. It was my gain, mine and your dad's. And Marla's. Just think – if you hadn't grown up with us you'd never have met Marla.

So please be happy and continue to be the wonderful man you are. Consider what a tortured life Grace has led all these years whether or not she acknowledges it. No woman can deny her child the way she has without causing disfiguring and scarring in her heart and soul. Maybe you can actually help to heal her, if you travel the path to her.

Also – rave about Marla's cooking. I know she'll want these recipes. That's why I left these notes there!

I'll be looking down from on high or looking up from below. Wherever I end up, I'll always be part of all three of your lives. Take care of your dad. There's so much to say. I hope I've said it to you enough – I love you seems to say it all.

Love,

Mom

Marla's faint cough reminded him that she was in the room with her note, too. When he turned, he saw her wiping the tears at the same moment she saw him wiping his.

At dinner, Vern told James about the letters. "In the recipe box, huh? She had the right take on all of us." He took a sip of wine and nudged Marmalade off his foot under the table. He picked the kitten up and hugged him. "She left mine by the coffee grinder. I figure she was giving herself a week to get out of the hospital, and if she didn't make it, knew that eventually I'd be grinding up some more beans." He put the wriggling cat back down and wiping his eyes, said, "If she got back before then, she'd have taken the note and ripped it up."

Fran Hasson

BOOK TWO

Fran Hasson

Chapter 13

Ye are fallen from grace
Galatians 5:4

WHAT THE HELL IS GOING ON? thought Grace. Why now, after all these years? What ever gave him the idea to look for me?

She sank heavily onto the sofa, looked out over the valley, and lit a cigarette. The plume of smoke found a wisp of the trade wind and floated away from the verandah. Two ponies below her house neighed into the wind and frolicked around the corral, stamping and blowing, kicking up clouds of dirt that obscured the stable behind them. They reminded her of the Chincoteague ponies from one of her previous residences.

How much farther away could I have run? she thought. I guess I knew this day would come but I'd have thought it much sooner. He's nearly forty years old now. Has he tried before to find me? If so, I never heard about it.

Fuck him. I won't see him. He ruined my life once, twice, actually, and he's not going to ruin it now. How can I tell my kids? And what about George? How can I ever explain Vern to them? She took a deep drag of her cigarette and let the smoke out slowly. She crossed and uncrossed her legs. The dogs let out a chorus of howls. "For God's sake, shut up!" she screamed at them. Ordinarily their barking didn't affect her like this. She didn't mind the ruckus they made for she figured it would dissuade anyone from intruding into the remote home she shared with her husband.

They had moved into the island retreat three years ago. This was their fifth move in the twenty-five years they had been married. George didn't understand her need to change locations, but knew when she exhibited signs of the wanderlust - the nervous edge that would develop in her voice, the cleaning out of books, clothes, pictures every few years – that she would soon be whining about being closed in, that she needed a new start.

She couldn't tell him that she'd had nightmares for years. Many times the chubby little boy would reach out his hands and call for her, "Mommy, don't leave me." Sometimes she'd see his anguished face as her car sped away. Often he followed her, his little legs pumping, tears streaming down his cheeks. Other times she pictured him as a tall, lithe, handsome young man in cap and gown holding a college diploma, pointing a finger at her in the audience and telling the assembled crowd, "There's the woman who threw me away. Shame on you, Grace Bjork." When she'd awaken, she would calm herself down, reassured that at least he didn't know her married name, that she was now Grace Elsmere.

She couldn't tell her husband that she was afraid he'd turn up some day on her doorstep and that she would recognize him although he could no longer resemble the two-year- old boy she'd last seen when she left him with Jane.

How had he found Jane, Grace wondered. And what would Jane tell him now? Would she lead him to St. Croix? Would the dogs' barking signal his arrival on the rutted dirt road that ran alongside her house? Would he walk up the path that led from the riding academy below and see her sitting on her verandah before she could hide herself? Would they have to move again so soon? She was starting to feel like she'd found a place where she could be safe forever.

George loved it here. His old job as boat surveyor along the Eastern Shore had been readily transferrable to the Virgin Islands. He had more than enough work to keep him busy, in fact had thought he would be retiring on this exotic island. Word of mouth had led scores of boaters to him. He was sought after at the St. Croix Yacht Club, which Grace had joined with him. He was happy that she had finally joined an organization with him after all these years. She had always been interested in the children's activities, had baked cookies for Joe's Cub Scout pack, attended every PTA meeting, went to all Sally's plays and recitals, sat in the bleachers at Joe's and Deb's athletic events, in short – anything involving their three children. Now, after twenty-five years, Grace was a bona fide partner to George. New friends they had formed on the island said, "If you see one, you'll see the other." They played Team Trivia at Pelican Cove, sailed their twenty- foot catamaran together, held parties at their spacious home overlooking Buck Island. They were becoming more popular by the week.

She stubbed her cigarette out on a conch shell and walked through the French doors into the kitchen. Smelling the frangipani wafting through the side door and listening to the palm fronds brush the gate to the carport, she resolved to stay put, to remain here. Jane surely wouldn't tell him where she was and even if she did, what were the chances he'd come this far to see her when she had told Jane bluntly that she didn't want any contact with him?

The tiniest of the three dogs, the Yorkie, Tiger, bounded playfully toward her. She picked up the furry bundle and turned him over, bringing him over her shoulders and burying her face into his wriggling belly. "I wish I loved people like I love you," she cooed into his ears which were standing straight up as if to catch every word from her adoring mouth.

She held onto this thought. She had always had a propensity for caring for animals. They gave unconditional love without ever asking for anything in return. A one-sided love affair. Sure she loved her husband and her three children and cared for them. She felt she was a good mother. But the deepest part of her knew that she would never ignore a cat that came meowing in the cold of winter or a dog that had been left off by some owner who no longer wanted it. She would take it in and care for it until she could find a home for it. Why was she able to jettison Vern the way she did, shedding not one tear the last time she left him with her sister, and hesitating not one second to give her power of attorney to allow that couple to adopt him?

She settled in on the macramé hammock on the verandah, snuggling with Tiger. He allowed her to cradle him and burrowed in to her for an afternoon nap. As she stroked him to sleep, she thought of how quickly she had handed Vern back to the nurse when she first brought him in after the painful and lengthy ordeal of childbirth. The nurse's broad smile had disappeared, was replaced with a questioning frown, and she retreated hugging the newborn close to her. Grace overheard her telling another nurse that that was the earliest case of postpartum depression she'd ever heard of.

The phone rang, startling Tiger, who scampered from the hammock, his claws ripping a small tear in Grace's arm as he sped away. As she clapped her hand over the scratch, Grace muttered, "I gotta get George to clip those nails." She cradled the phone against her shoulder while she wiped the wound with a wet paper towel. "Hi Jane," she said into the phone. "What good tidings of glad joy are you bringing me today?"

Jane reported her conversation with Vern. "Really, Grace, he sounds like a gentleman. He wants to meet you. He says he won't cause you any problems."

"No problems?" Grace searched through the cabinet by the phone for a Band-Aid. "Jane. Now really. Do you want to break the news to George and my kids about this brother, about George's stepson?"

Her voice started to border on hysteria and Jane quickly tried to defuse the situation. "OK, I know it will be hard, but can't we gradually bring it up?"

"Oh sure. Tonight at dinner I'll lay the groundwork. By the way, George – did you know I've been concealing a secret ever since I met you? Why no, Grace, what is it?" she said in a gravely tone. "Well, how about if I tell you a little more tomorrow night?" She glared into the phone and spat out, "Do you think that'll work?"

"Look, I know you've been keeping this to yourself, but aren't you curious about him?"

"Frankly, no. Great – he's led a good life, I suppose – the *gentleman*. And it's been without any input from me. So let's just keep it that way."

"You'll be sorry someday. Now that he is on the lookout, I'll bet he'll find you. And I might as well let you know, I *am* going to meet him. I'm having him here this summer. Also – I'm inviting my kids, his cousins. They deserve to meet him and so do your kids. Grace, they're his half-brother and sisters."

"Don't you *dare* invite my kids to meet him!"

"Would you really cut me out of your life if I did?"

"I cut him out, didn't I?"

"I've always wondered how you were able to do that. Haven't you ever thought of him all these years? I'd have been so curious and so happy if he found me – which, of course he has – but if he were my son, I would be on the first plane to see him."

"Look, Jane, you're you and I'm me. This is not the only difference we've had over the years. I don't want to talk about him, OK?"

"OK, for now, but I know there will be more."

*****

Grace walked the length of the house facing the road. She watered the poinsettia bushes, the asparagus fern, the periwinkle, and the variegated coleus that provided a lush setting for the lilac house with the lime green shutters. She walked around to the side entrance where her garden was located and got to work weeding and watering. The care of her garden and plants soothed her. While she didn't want to think of Vern, his image kept popping into her mind as she pruned the lime tree and pulled weeds from the base of her tomato plants. She dropped a tomato hornworm into the pail of soapy water she used as her "insecticide," drowning some of her anxiety along with it. Why did he have to come into her life now? she asked herself again. She wondered what he looked like as an adult. Did he resemble her? Did he look more like his father? Whichever brother that was…

The memory of that night after a relative's wedding caused her to puncture the tomato she was removing from its stem. Juice sprayed her face. Tiger bounced around her, whimpering and clawing his way up her side, trying to lick the tomato juice. She nudged him away as scenes poured in: Vern and Tom, Jane's brothers-in-law, were drinking boilermakers with her. One thing led to another. The memories flashed back. Vern, the older brother on top of her, Tom, the younger one, pleading, "Aw, c'mon Vern. When's it my turn?"

171

Grace, giggling, fumbling for Vern's zipper, groping for his penis, directing it toward her and calling out, "Hurry up – I want to see Tom's!" The next morning. The hangover, the knowledge of what they'd done. The following month – the missed menstrual period and the certainty that Ted, her husband, who was fighting rebels in Vietnam, would never forgive her.

Her family thought she had named the infant Vernon Thomas in honor of the two brothers who were killed three months after the incident in a car wreck. The brothers were both drunk and returning from a night of vigorous partying in nearby Pasadena. Only Grace knew she'd named him that because she wasn't sure which brother was the father and she wanted the names to be a reminder to her of what could happen.

It was a mistake to have called him Vernon Thomas, but birth certificates were filled out immediately following births then, and in addition to the grim reminder the labels provided, Grace thought she could raise the child and that the names would link them to the family. She knew she would need support and hoped she could find it from the family. She had not realized that his little heart-shaped earlobe would prove to be an obstacle. It turned out that her niece, Pru, had one, too. So did Bert, Jane's husband. There had been innuendoes and Jane's outright accusation that Grace had had an affair with her husband. Grace wondered if both brothers had such an earlobe. Although she remembered details of the romping and feverish sex play, she had no recollection of specific facial features of the men. When Jane questioned the aberrant earlobe, Grace had flippantly explained that Bert Seaman obviously was not the only man that had heart-shaped earlobes in his semen. The brothers' names never came up, so Grace assumed the hereditary trait might have skipped them.

*****

That night Grace and George went to dinner and Team Trivia. She was pre-occupied with thoughts of Vern and the fear he might intrude upon her life, the way he had almost forty years earlier. George noticed she was not paying attention to the questions.

"Are you OK?" he asked. "You seem distracted, not your usual self."

It was true. Usually she was at the edge of her seat, ready to huddle and offer an answer or agree or disagree with the group's decision. She sipped her rum and Coke, stirred the ice with the swizzle stick, ordered another and chain-smoked. When she noticed a few on her team blowing the smoke away with their hands, she glared at them, a signal to George that they probably needed to leave early. Grace was the only smoker in the entire group of eight. She often thought the new crowd of friends they had made only accepted her because of George. She was right. They tolerated her smoke and capitalized on her humor, her willingness to try anything, and her love of animals. Above all they accepted her because they all liked George. He was a rock, knew boats, and offered a helping hand to anyone who needed a ride, help with painting or repairing a boat. She knew he also enjoyed a beer in the afternoon at Ziggy's, and was a typical island man.

He leaned close to her and said," How about if we go home now? You look pretty beat."

On the way home, George tried to pry out of her what the problem was, but Grace just told him, "I'm tired. Too much sun today, I guess. I did a lot of yardwork."

George let it go at that. "Maybe a good night's rest will solve the problem," he said.

A good night's rest was not to be had. She tossed and turned, eventually ended up on the sofa on the verandah with a glass of wine and her pack of Marlboros. When George padded out to see what the problem was, he hesitated to disturb her. Her glance was far away, extending beyond the valley, past the rolling hills, beyond Buck Island. He went back to bed. Grace never noticed him because she was playing back the scene when her husband Ted had returned from Vietnam, word for word, each expression as vivid and contorted, the fear as palpable as it was that day:

She remembered the hall door clicking open and how she quickly settled the baby in his bassinette and hurried toward the door. Ted pushed past her, shoving his duffel bag into her, knocking her off balance against the wall.

"Is he here?" he asked as he dropped the heavy bag behind the sofa.

"What do you mean?"

"What the fuck do you think I mean?" His face twisted as he spat out the words. He moved closer, within inches of her face. "Maybe I shoulda said They, are they here. Your bastard and its father!" Spit erupted as his rage heightened. He clenched his fists, then jammed them into his khaki pockets.

She straightened herself and smoothed her housedress, catching her bandaged hand against the torn pocket. She looked at her hand and patted the adhesive tape tighter against her skin. Her downcast eyes turned toward his red face. Quietly she said, "You make it sound—"

"Sound like what? Like you're a fuckin' whore?"

"Ted, I don't know what to say. I was lonely."

"Lonely? And I guess there was nothing to do but fuck around while I was running from napalm bombs and gooks who wired their kids to blow us up? Make you *sound* like a whore?" He looked around the apartment, furtively, as though preparing for hand-to-hand combat. "I've always called a spade a spade."

A soft, whining cry sounded from the bedroom. "Is that your love child? I guess you expect me to go and coo and chuck him under his chin?" His face reddened again, the cords in his neck straining against his Army issue T-shirt and khaki blouse, the pocket festooned with campaign ribbons, highlighted by the purple heart ribbon in the upper of the two rows. His entire body tensed as he turned toward the sound.

She put her hand out to stop him from going to the child. "He's an innocent baby. You can't be angry with him. He's not at fault."

The tension eased in his body. "Maybe he's not. But what do you expect me to do now? What a great hero's welcome this is. Half the country spits at us and here I am in my castle, a man's castle... Ha! And who's here to greet me? My loving wife and someone else's bastard!"

"Ted, you don't need to use that word for the baby. We need to work this out. Start over." Grace looked toward the bedroom. "Can you give him a chance?"

"Give him a chance, give you a chance. Give me a break! I took my chances in Nam and I made it back, but I'm not taking any more chances with you and certainly not with that little bawler in there." He moved to the couch and sank into the deep cushion. He covered his face with both hands and massaged his temples, digging into his scalp as he worked his way over his head. Leaning back, he looked at his wife sitting across from him. "Who's the father?" he asked, the tone steely, matching his penetrating stare.

Her face jerked toward the window as though a rope had tightened about her neck. She felt trapped, wished she were at the gallows, wished the hangman would open the trapdoor and remove her from this moment. She faced him, her mouth a thin, tight line of determination. "We need to raise him together no matter who the father is."

"*We?*" His eyes narrowed and the redness in his face began to rise again. "We?" He moved toward her in a crouched position, elbows bent and hands curled. She thought he was going to reach for her and strangle her. Instead he stopped short and thrust his face close to hers, spitting with rage again. "You probably don't even know who the father is, you dirty slut!" He slammed his open hand across her cheek, his violence seeming to awaken something inside of him. He recoiled and backed off. He lowered his voice, although now it was trembling, the rage still not having been spent. "There is no *we*." More quietly he added, "Y'know, Grace, I'm not even sure there ever was a *we*." He stood and went behind the couch, picked up his duffel bag, and started for the door. "I'm going to my brother's house. Tomorrow I'll come back for my things and move them to his place. What time will you and the baby be out?" He drew out the word baby in a sarcastic tone and motioned to the bedroom where the child had begun wailing for attention. "That's where you belong now, not with me."

"But, Ted," she pleaded, "can't we do something – can't we start over?"

"I am starting over, Grace, but not with you." He continued to the door and left her standing there, the baby's wailing growing more insistent.

*****

Grace started to cry. Tiger jumped onto her lap and Ginger, the golden retriever, settled against her leg, nuzzling her and staring up with watery brown eyes as her tail thumped softly against the wooden floor. I guess that's when I first began to really hate my baby, Grace recalled. She had thought Ted might soften when he saw him, held him. Ted was a good man. Boring as hell but a good man. Even though she knew he'd never forgive her, she believed the baby would win him over.

She recalled how she resented Vern's appearance in the world, how the social worker at the hospital had assured her that her feelings were valid but convinced her to give the baby a chance. He told her that her life was not ruined, that a whole new life could include this innocent child. In the few months before Ted returned, she had bonded with her baby. She enjoyed his smell, his hearty laugh which revealed the toothless gums, the tiny toes and fingers which she took into her mouth whenever she bathed him, his softness, his dependence on her. This dependence became a burden when Ted so viciously cast them out of his life. Vern became a constant reminder of her iniquitous behavior with the Seaman brothers.

Her soft crying increased to sobs. The sound traveled the length of the verandah to the bedroom where George heard her. He had been lying awake since he had discovered her on the sofa. Now he had to act; this was something that could not be ignored. He came out onto the verandah but Grace did not even notice him. Her face was in her hands and her body wracked. The Golden retriever moved aside as George jockeyed into position next to her. Tiger growled at him, alerting Grace to his presence. She wiped her nose on her sleeve and sniffed, raked her eyes and cheeks with both hands and said nothing.

"Grace, what is it? You haven't been yourself this whole day."

She became defensive. "It's nothing," she said. "Maybe just a little postmenopausal PMS."

George knew this side of Grace. This was how their need to move had always started - with these moods, which always heightened into the behaviors she dismissed as the wanderlust. But now George had decided he was staying on St. Croix, with or without Grace. "I wish you'd share this with me," he said. "You know - we've been married twenty-five years. Doesn't that count for something?"

She stiffened as she reached for her unfinished wine. She lit a cigarette, which she knew would drive George back into the house. Predictably, he rose and retreated. He turned and said, "Y'know, in our twenty-five years together, I've picked up on the *Let me light a cigarette and get rid of George* thing you do. Grace, I think it's time we made a change in our lives."

She swallowed the wine hard and coughed, fear gripping her. Her defenses immediately took over. After taking a drag and blowing the smoke in George's direction, she challenged him. "Yeah? And what does that mean?"

"Right now you're upset. This thing that's bothering you - " He moved back, a little closer to her and said gently, "Think about it. If you can't share it with me, why? Who can you share it with?"

"Not everything needs to be shared," she retaliated. "I don't expect you to tell *me* everything."

"If I had something that drove me the way this thing is driving you and I couldn't share it with you, I'd have to wonder about us. Don't you trust me?"

She pulled the afghan up and lay back. "Can we talk about this tomorrow?" There was a note of conciliation in her voice, a suggestion of resignation and despair, which George seemed to perceive.

George went back to bed. While he tossed and turned, Grace considered her options. She held Tiger close as he whined and snuggled, pawing at her face gently. This time Grace sobbed so quietly into her tiny dog that George couldn't hear her, even as he lay wide awake.

*****

The next morning she made coffee and they sat at the slab dining table. George had designed and constructed it from a piece of wood he'd purchased from the Mahogany LEAP, a popular local shop in the Rainforest. He faced the valley and she sat across from him, facing the kitchen.

"Feel better this morning?" he asked.

She cradled the coffee mug in both hands and glanced toward the side of the house which faced the pool. Her defensive tone was back. "George, this involves something that happened long before I met you and doesn't concern you." She stared across at him. "I hope you won't bug me about it."

"There's where you're wrong," he answered. "Anything that affects you that much does involve me." His voice was gentle and his eyes pleaded with her.

She averted her glance, knowing that his soft brown eyes would be hard to resist. He drained his coffee and went into the kitchen for a refill, bringing the pot back. She watched him, his athleticism surfacing as he stepped over Tiger while balancing the pot and his mug. He motioned to her and set it on the table when she refused more. "This thing that bothers you – is this the reason we've been moving every few years?"

Her eyes widened in fear, fear that he was on to something. Had Jane called him and told him? "Why should it have anything to do with the moves? You wanted to go, too."

"Really? I wanted to change jobs, move the kids away from their schools and friends? *They* wanted to go?" The pleading look in his eyes had turned into an angry look which bored into Grace.

"You never complained."

"I should have."

"Then why didn't you?"

George stood and walked to the wooden rail, leaned on it and looked down into the valley. "You were always like those ponies down there. You wanted to be free." He turned to her. "I guess I was afraid you'd leave us."

"What kind of a woman did you think I was?" Then the truth hit her. She was that woman, a woman who would leave her family.

"Let's just say I didn't want to put you to the test. But I won't move again. I wish you'd share this with me." He came back to the table and sat. "I've seen this mood change every time you forced us to go. This time, you'll have to go it alone. I'm staying here."

She bent her head and stared into her coffee, then stood and walked to the rail facing the pool. "I have to trim the bougainvillea today."

George realized the conversation had ended. "I have a boat to survey at the Club this morning." He was not content to drop the subject. He added, "There's a good psychologist in Christiansted. Her name is Padereau, Marcia Padereau, I believe." He said to her back, "For yourself and our marriage, I wish you'd give her a call." With that, he took his cup inside and readied himself for work.

*****

The orange honeysuckle had trailed into the bougainvillea and was so intertwined and hard to separate that Grace had to use the machete to hack sections clear. She threw the clippings over the side of the wall into the bush. Just like I threw Vern away, she thought. Vern. Vern. Vern. No matter what she did, no matter what she looked at, Vern's image transposed itself. She saw him shaking his crib, standing on tiptoes, trying to reach her. She saw him dragging his stuffed shark around. Grace's mother had bought it for him after having read the thriller, *Jaws*. He'd called the toy *Choss*, and carried it everywhere he went. It was his one source of stability for far too long.

Her relentless dwelling on him had permeated her entire being now. She sat at the edge of the pool and rippled the water with her feet. Watching the waves race to the center, she decided she should call the psychologist.

*****

"What brings you here?" asked the psychologist two days later. "What can I help you with?"

Grace pulled her Marlboros out of her canvas bag but was interrupted by Dr. Padereau. "I'm sorry, but this is a non-smoking area. This whole building is non-smoking. Can you abstain for an hour?"

Grace looked out at the turquoise waters, at the sprawling Hotel-on-the-Cay, the Sunfish sails flapping in the breeze. She took in a deep audible breath that she exhaled disgustedly. "Rules, rules, everywhere. If you can't smoke at a shrink's office, where in the …dickens… can you?"

"We seem to be getting off on a stumbling foot," the psychologist said. "Let's just pretend we're on an airplane flying to New York. You couldn't smoke there, could you?" She extended a dish toward Grace. "Gum? Candy, with or without sugar? A glass of water? Can I give you a substitute?"

Grace leaned back in her chair. This is bullshit, she thought. Why did I even come here?

"Let's start over. Good afternoon. My name is Marcia. Are you called Grace or would you prefer Ms. or Mrs. Elsmere?"

Grace had to crack a smile. "OK. OK. I'm Grace and I'm here, I don't know quite why."

"I guess it's not to quit smoking…" Marcia arched an eyebrow as she leaned toward Grace.

Grace liked her humor. "No. My husband said I should come."

"Do you agree?"

"Maybe."

"Well, how about if we start with why he suggested it."

Grace told her how he'd discovered her on the verandah sobbing her head off. "He wanted to know why and I told him I couldn't talk about it," she admitted.

"Can you talk to me about it? You do know that anything you say here is confidential."

Grace hunched her shoulders and leaned forward, almost assuming a fetal position. In a little-girl voice, she said, "I gave up my child almost forty years ago." She looked down at her clenched fists. "And now he's trying to find me." She surprised herself by blurting this out. It was the first time anyone other than her sister knew about her releasing Vern.

"It's not just that I gave him up," she continued. "I was glad to let my sister adopt him out, to take care of my problem." She covered her face and cried into her hands. "That's how I saw him – as a problem."

Marcia Padereau came from behind her desk and poured a glass of water for Grace. "Take your time," she said and returned to her seat.

The two exchanged questions and answers, Grace filling her in on events of the sordid past and recent happenings with Pru and Jane. "How can I tell George? How can I tell my kids?"

The hour was nearly up and the therapist had other clients waiting. She made an appointment for Monday. "Perhaps you can let George know you're working on the problem. Do you think he'll give you space? That he can understand without knowing the details?"

"George has put up with my nonsense for twenty-five years. If ever a man deserved a halo, it's him."

Marcia laughed at that but added, "It sounds to me like you've punished yourself for a long time. I imagine you've given George a lot of yourself that you're not taking credit for."

Grace considered this. But the balance sheet between what she'd given George and the kids fell way short of what she'd done to Vern, she thought.

Marcia peered at her and said, "Do you think that's a fair statement?"

"I'll think about that over the weekend, too."

"Another important thing to think about, and we'll discuss it next time, is the fact that you really *are* a human being. People make mistakes." She stood and walked over to the window and held the ornamental wrought iron bars. The shutters were open wide, letting the trade wind circulate through the room. "I wish I didn't have another client right this minute. I'd be down there getting a beef paté."

Grace gathered her bag and held her Marlboros in her hand. "I'll be down there before your next client comes in and this will be my beef paté," she said as she held the pack up.

*****

That weekend Grace and George went to the yacht club for Sunday brunch. Grace's mood had been lighter and she found herself thinking of ways she could tell George, not ways of hiding it, not ways of excoriating herself. She thought she had to find the right time, the right approach. This was a step forward because she had never considered revealing this deep dark secret life she'd led. They sat with another couple who'd lived on the island for a number of years.

When Grace lit her first cigarette, she noticed Audrey's glance at her husband. Audrey coughed and Grace excused herself from the table, walked to the edge of the pavilion and looked out at the numerous luxury yachts, catamarans, and other vessels berthed at the marina. She blew clouds of smoke, looking back at the table from time to time. She detected an air of triumph from Audrey and noticed that the three were engaged in lively conversation. The awareness of how her smoking affected the others crept up her neck and the next inhalation caught halfway, causing her to flick the cigarette away and double over, coughing. When she returned to the table after coughing the last offending strains of smoke out, George asked, "Are you OK?"

"Yeah, just allergies kicking in."

"The smoking probably doesn't help," Audrey offered.

Grace glared at her. The message received, she continued, "You're probably, right." She wanted to add, "Ms Know-it-all," but simply smiled and said, "I'll take that under advisement." She could hardly wait to tell Marcia how she'd restrained herself. They had talked about her compulsiveness, how that had often offended people. How her restlessness had led her to wandering, to placing Vern in others' care, how she had allowed instant gratification to rule her life far too often. She would not have started an argument with Audrey, would not have called her a name, but previous to her first counseling session, she would never have added a conciliatory remark, either. She patted herself on the back and noted that she was truly aware of how offensive her smoking was. Looking around the club, she noticed that not one member was smoking. So what, she thought. But this was another addition to her new consciousness.

After brunch, they took Audrey and Steve out for a ride on the catamaran. Audrey was an expert at sailing: she helped George with lifting anchor, hoisting the sail, and coming about as they made their way to the underwater national park surrounding Buck Island. On the way, a schooner was heading across their bow even though they had the right of way. Audrey, with smooth facility, helped to tack to avoid a collision. Her suppleness and skill impressed George. Grace watched as his eyes studied the young woman's body the way they did every feature of a boat he surveyed, missing no small detail. A twinge of jealousy shook her. What would her life be like without George? What did she really offer him? Had he deferred to her all these years, asking for nothing in return? Was he like the animals she loved so much, giving unconditional love? She sat on the hull watching the capable Audrey doing what *she* should be doing, helping her husband and Steve manage the cat.

It registered in her mind that Audrey and Steve were around Vern's age. Vern and what was her name – Molly, Mary, Marcia? No. Marcia was her therapist. She wondered if Vern had children. She would ask Jane for a little more information about him.

This struck her as odd, that she should be questioning Vern's life. How had she so effectively blocked him out all these years? Now that he was trying to find her, she thought about him all the time. When Jane asked if she was curious, she really wasn't. Over the years he meant no more to Grace than did the maître d' at the Yacht Club, than the salesman at Home Depot who advised her on gardening supplies. In fact they were more important to her life than Vern. She had contact with her own children - how strange, *her own children*, she thought, as though Vern was not hers – on a weekly basis. The telephone system on St. Croix was very expensive regarding calls *to* the States, but her three made calls *from* the States to her regularly, at least once a week for the girls and about every other week for Joe.

She remembered her move to St. Croix and experiencing the first phone disruption, the first power outage, the first time she couldn't find a box of Cheerios anywhere on the island. She had become so accustomed to the many little obstacles that had irritated her, that she was now able to consider them as such trivial setbacks. She felt that she had grown so much since arriving on the tiny island, that her life had begun over. But there was still Vern following her all these years. She had thought of him whenever the nightmares came. But in recent years those frightful dreams occurred less frequently. Now when she was free of childcare and was developing a life for herself, now that the nightmares had stopped torturing her, Vern was imposing himself upon her again.

So deep in thought she was that when Audrey called out, "Coming about!" she didn't hear her. George was close enough and saw what was happening. He was able to push her out of the way before the boom crashed into her.

When they dropped anchor at Buck Island, George and Grace stayed onboard while the younger pair snorkeled. They went below in the port hull where George made drinks. "You were pretty wrapped up in something a while ago. Nearly got yourself killed."

"Yeah. That's what thinking does for you."

They went topside with their drinks and sat beneath the limp blue and white spinnaker. "Is the counseling doing any good?" George asked.

"We'll see."

"Still can't talk about it, huh?"

Grace shot back, "I thought what I said there was confidential."

George clammed up. He rose, went to the back of the boat and fussed around with some of the rigging, holding his drink in one hand and testing the tension with the other. She noticed how, although he was in his early sixties, George's body was toned and hard, the white chest hairs and crow's feet wrinkles around his eyes and mouth betraying his age. His dark brown hair was graying at the temples, adding a dignity to his kind face.

I've done it again, thought Grace. He's a good man. Why can't I just tell him? She justified her reticence by remembering how long she'd held this secret. She knew George would accept her even if he couldn't understand how she'd cordoned Vern off so successfully for so long. She had been a good mother, she reminded herself, to her three children. She recounted the list of things she'd done over the years, not just the attendance at events – the special birthday cakes, the night she slept on the floor so Deb wouldn't roll out of bed onto the humidifier, the piles of admission sheets and brochures she went through as each child neared college age. The list went on and on. That has to count for something, doesn't it? she thought.

*****

At the conclusion of her fourth session with Marcia, Grace said she was ready to call Jane and ask for more details about Vern. She still wasn't ready to meet him or tell her family about him. "This is a giant step," Marcia told her, "this gathering information about your son. Let me know how it goes."

Your son. Grace rolled this around in her brain as she walked down Church Street to the boardwalk. She sat on a bench by the ferry and thought of the words *your son.* For almost twenty-five years her conscious mind had only thought of Joe as her son. When Joe was born, she thought of Vern but had quickly banished him from her consideration. After all, he was dead and buried somewhere in Ohio. She had refused to acknowledge him. He had remained in that corner of her brain except when he surfaced in her nightmares. Now *your son* took on a new dimension. If she agreed to meet him, would he accuse her of being the unfeeling, almost criminal mother that she was to him? Or would he want to know how she had grown to love him in the few months before Ted called him a bastard and then left her? Would he understand how the men who followed dumped her the minute they discovered this fatherless child? NO, she couldn't meet him.

Her resolve to ask Jane failed ... for the second time since she had heard the news that he was looking for her.

*****

She examined the frangipani, looking for the strange caterpillars that chewed the leaves. She used to pick them off and drown them before she was told the leaves would fall off anyway and the frangipani would temporarily resemble a hurricane-blown bunch of sticks.

190

Black and white were the caterpillars. How orderly the world would be if everything were black or white, she thought. No right or wrong. Just black or white. The sweet odor of the jasmine soothed her as she walked to her garden at the side of the house. She cut some bok choy and kale and plucked two tomatoes.

She went inside through the guest bedroom door and heard the phone ringing. When she saw that it was Jane, she decided not to pick up. Jane would just have news of Vern. Their reunion dinner was coming up next week. She knew Jane was trying to get her to come but she had told her she absolutely would not. She didn't want to hear about the reunion. She definitely did not want to hear any last-ditch pleas to allow her children to come and meet Vern. She knew Jane wouldn't invite them without her permission and decided it was better not to answer the phone.

After she washed her vegetables and covered them with water, threw in her fresh herbs and some potatoes and set the pot to simmer, she dialed the voice mail. The tone of Jane's voice startled her. "Grace, please call me. I just talked to Vern. He had some news that was pretty upsetting."

She nearly dropped the phone. She gripped tighter, her hand trembling slightly. Now what could *that* be, thought Grace. Has he found out where I live? Is he coming here? Did something happen to him? She was surprised at her reaction to her last question. It never before occurred to her that she would care if he suffered any misfortune. In fact there were times since discovering he wanted to meet her that she had wished he really was dead and buried in Ohio. Now, she found herself concerned. Not to the degree she would have if it had been her own children. There it was again - her own children. Vern was her own child, too. She really needed to face up to it. She pushed the speed dial for Jane but pushed "off" before it could ring. No, I still can't do it, she said to herself.

BOOK THREE

Fran Hasson

Chapter 14

*'Tis known by the name of perseverance in a good cause
– and of obstinacy in a bad one.*
Lauren e Sterne, *Tristram Shandy*

A YEAR PASSED. Life for Vern and Marla was changed in that James had sold the home in Vero Beach and bought a small condo in their complex. They had considered moving to make more room for him, but James decided he could build a new life with the daily contact he enjoyed with them. He even bought a litter pan and kept Marmalade with him when the two traveled and sometimes during the day when Marla needed to stay for student conferences. Vern and Marla visited his aunt and cousins throughout the year and now included James in some of the trips to Maryland. Vern had made no further attempt to locate Grace, but the urge was returning.

One night at dinner he said to Marla and James, "It's about time we made a return trip to St. Croix, don't you think?"

"This is pretty sudden," said Marla. "What's the matter? Cold weather starting to get you down?"

It was mid-December. The weather was beginning to chill in the Mid-Atlantic region. The leaves had fallen outside their breakfast nook, squirrels were scampering around the deck searching for the nuts that Marla threw out for them – preparing for the winter famine, and the duck hunters had shot their first quarries that morning.

Vern had a faraway look as he scraped the last of the mashed potatoes from the bowl. "I guess with Christmas coming, I was thinking of the perfect gift – Christmas on St. Croix. Rosalie always said what a festive time that was. We could all stay with her and visit our old friends there." He rubbed his left earlobe and added, "It's been over six years now...."

"Don't count me in," said James. "Someone needs to spend the holiday with Marmalade." The cat lay on his foot under the table and rubbed against his leg at the mention of his name.

"Someone needs to spend the holiday with you, too," said Marla. "Maybe we could go after the new year. Rosalie has also talked about the Three Kings Day Parade, which is a big deal there." She looked under the table at the purring cat. "We could get Sybil to watch the baby and we'll all go."

"An even better idea," agreed Vern.

"You wouldn't be interested in looking for Grace, would you?" James asked, his eyes twinkling. "If you are, don't tiptoe around it. You know your mother was eager for you to connect with her to satisfy your curiosity. And I'll need a little rest after the holiday." He hoisted the cat onto his lap. "No stranger's gonna take care of MY kitty," he said. "We're staying together!"

They discussed how, over the past year, the subject had pretty much been put on the back burner. Grace's continued, adamant refusal and the family's reluctance to broach the subject, along with Katherine's death and the period of grieving, had put a halt to any active search.

Relieved to have the subject out on the table, Vern started to clear the dishes. Refreshing everyone's wine, he proposed a toast. "Here's to round two of the search." After he took a sip, he said, "I'm still not sure I want to meet her but I really *do* want to see her."

After dinner, they walked James home. It had become their concession to exercising. Vern was so busy at work that he had given up on going to the gym, Marla had never been an enthusiast of working out, and this added time together pleased the three of them. It also comforted Vern to look out after his father. He felt he was honoring his mother by doing this. James's condo was just around the corner from theirs but in the same building. They could look down from their deck and see him sitting on his back screened porch below. Marla often stood on the deck with her cell phone and waved down to James, who loved to sit and listen to the fountains on the lagoon.

"So you really think Mom would be happy that I'm doing this?" he said to James as they were ready to leave him.

"I know she would," James assured him.

*****

Marla phoned her friend on St. Croix as soon as they returned home. "How's the McGee B&B? Any room in the inn for wayward travelers?" she asked.

"Don't tell me? Are you finally coming? When? For how long?" Rosalie's questions came nonstop. "Oliver's dancing around and around! He knows!" Oliver was the shaggy dog that had taken to Vern, trailing him everywhere he went like Mary's little lamb.

"Yeah, right," said Marla, rolling her eyes and smiling at Vern, who was grinning as he listened to the speakerphone.

"Besides seeing everyone, we want to follow up on the mystery mother we told you about last year," said Vern.

"I checked up on her and I'm sure we can arrange a meeting."

"No. I just want to see her, not meet her."

"Still doesn't want to meet you?"

"I'm afraid not." He twisted his earlobe.

"Mother of the year," said Rosalie.

"Of the century," put in Marla.

"Anyway," resumed Vern, can you find her haunts, maybe someplace where we could just sit and observe her?"

Rosalie said, "Her husband, George, takes his computer, laptop, and iPhone to Darryl all the time. He found out they live right up the street from Ziggy's. George goes there nearly every day. It's a popular little place – gas station/meeting place/grocery store/restaurant – an all-around neighborhood hangout. He's real popular with everyone there and at the yacht club. I'm sure my snoops can ferret out some info. Too bad you can't jet on down here right now for a piña colada. Guess who's whipping them up for me? We're expecting guests any minute now." Vern could picture her straightening cushions on her rattan sofa and taking some coasters from the side table. He remembered how she placed them strategically around the grouping of sofa and chairs on the verandah when they stayed with her before.

A male voice boomed out, "Takin' orders now, folks. What'll ya have?"

"Darryl! You dog! Are you ever coming back here?" Vern was animated.

"Not unless my future missus wants to. But why should she?"

Vern and Marla looked at each other, breaking into broad grins. "When's the big date? Are we invited? When did you pop the question?" They took turns firing questions, one after the other.

Plans were made with the dates set for the pair's visit. Rosalie and Darryl would be attending the Christmas party at the club. They were sure to see the Elsmeres there and possibly get an introduction.

"Don't get too chummy with them just yet," Vern cautioned. "Remember, I want to observe her without her knowing it."

*****

Vern was honoring his aunt's request to keep her out of it. He had not told Jane or her family of his St. Croix connections and would not tell them of this trip until after he'd taken it. It had been difficult leaving out this major incident in their lives as they had become closer and had shared stories. So many times he'd wanted to share the experience, especially with Jack, who was also a PADI-certified scuba diver, another of their shared interests. Deep down, Vern had known the time would come when they would visit the island and whether accidentally or on purpose, they would run into Grace. He felt it best to tell them after the fact, not have Jane fretting over Grace's response or whether or not to warn Grace in advance.

He envisioned times when they could go together with Jack and the family and have a scuba vacation. He would arrange it all with Bob, the divemaster he'd befriended. So many possibilities but one major stumbling block – Grace Elsmere. He'd even considered a family reunion with the whole crew of them taking over the island. They could rent one of the spacious homes sitting atop the rolling hills with views of the Caribbean. If only....

This trip would be the bellwether for him to know how to proceed with the Seaman family. He would tell them all about the trip the next time he was with them. They had invited him, Marla, and James for Christmas dinner. They hadn't committed yet. Now he would beg off, citing other plans for he knew his guilty conscience – or Marla's – would dictate spilling the beans about the upcoming trip.

Chapter 15

A friend is long sought, hardly found, and with difficulty kept.
St. Jerome, *Letter 1*

WAITING AT THE ARRIVALS LOUNGE was an entourage worthy of a visiting dignitary. Rosalie and Darryl, along with their friends Clemma Joseph and her daughter and son-in-law, Father Ambrose and his wife, and the dive crew stood to the side of a red carpet they'd rolled out to welcome Vern and Marla back to St. Croix.

Marla broke into tears as she tried to give group hugs to the little cluster. "I've missed you all so much," she said, sniffling and choking back the tears. Vern watched and shook his head as he passed through the crowd, shaking hands with them all.

"You'll get the chance to talk to everyone tonight. They're coming back to my place for dinner," Rosalie explained. Later, in the car, she told them that she and Darryl would be announcing their engagement at the welcome home dinner.

"That is, if it's OK with you. We don't want to steal your thunder by turning it into our celebration," Darryl said.

"She's really turning you into a gentleman," Vern joked. "I'd never have thought it possible." Leaning into the front seat, he said, "I can't think of a better time to announce it – a double celebration."

Diarra, Rosalie's assistant at her boutique shop, was catering the evening's meal. She and her husband were at the house making the preparations when the four returned from the airport. They settled into their room, showered and refreshed themselves, then sat on the verandah with Rosalie and Darryl. Oliver had picked up where he left off and was pressed into Vern's thigh, whining to be petted. Darryl and Vern talked about the computer businesses they both ran while Marla and Rosalie left to inspect the garden. The poinsettias were bright and colorful, displaying the various colors, some bright red, some pink, some a mixture. The bushes were as tall as Marla. "I sometimes wish we could live here," said Marla. "I've never gotten the feel and smell of the island out of my system. I feel like I'm home."

"You easily could be," said Rosalie. "Darryl could use competent help in his shop. And teachers are never in oversupply. Talk to Eulalie about it tonight. She could get you into a good position here."

"First of all, I don't think Vern could ever work for anyone. He really loves having his own business."

"Well, they could be partners. Darryl could continue at Gallows Bay and Vern could open up a branch in Frederiksted. People come from all over the island to Darryl. He's swamped. It would be good for both of them."

"Then there's my father-in-law. We can't desert him."

"Desert him? Bring him!"

"Something to think about. Let's see how it goes with the stranger-than-fiction mother of Vern." She spotted a chameleon darting through the bushes and laughed. "I'd forgotten about those little critters. Little Graces darting in and out of people's lives! I'd like to paint pictures of them all day long!"

"I'm sure that could be arranged, too. I think Vern would earn enough that you wouldn't have to teach. And you know you have a ready-made outlet for your artwork."

Marla remembered the boutique with the local artistry, designer clothes, and touristy items. It was a popular spot for shoppers coming off the cruise ships down the street from the classy shop.

Rosalie said, "Are we going to talk about your mission tonight? The others don't know about Vern's mother and her secret."

"I think it better if we don't. At least unless Vern is the one to bring it up. He's been so careful to keep her secret a secret, so I don't imagine he'd want to expose her here. Too many others could be hurt, starting with her husband."

The dinner was reminiscent of the birthday dinner Diarra had prepared for Vern when he turned thirty-five: A side table was heaped with island specialties: conch, baked fish, local lobster known as langouste, seasoned rice, pigeon peas, and side provisions of boiled plantain, lettuce, and tomatoes. This was Diarra's go-to meal for special occasions, and she had perfected it. Cruzan Rum cake was served on the verandah with coffee and after dinner drinks.

The welcoming committee was present for the meal. Everyone wanted to know what Vern and Marla had been doing since they had last seen them. They wanted Vern to bring his father on the next visit. "If we do that, we'll have to bring our cat along, too," said Marla. "They're inseparable."

"Marmalade can always stay here," Rosalie offered.

"With all these dogs? I don't think so." Marla looked around the verandah. Besides Oliver, who was still attached to Vern, there were two other devoted hounds who kept watch over Rosalie's home. They were keeping watch now over any crumbs that might fall their way.

One of the dogs, a short-haired, short-legged mongrel named Mister stood up and raced over to Darryl, who had moved to the center of the room. Mister sat up, waved his paws, and let out two shrill barks. "Thank you, Mister," he said, laughing as he reached for Rosalie, "for getting everyone's attention." The two stood together at the rail, facing the gathering of friends. "We have an announcement to make."

Chapter 16

Who sees with equal eye, as God of all,
A hero perish or a sparrow fall
Atoms or systems into ruin hurled
And now a bubble burst, and now a world.
Alexander Pope, *An Essay on Man*

THE CROWDS WERE SIX DEEP along King Street. As usual, the Three Kings Day Parade was two hours late getting started. In the meantime, the waiting spectators were patient. "Crucian time" was heard the length of the parade route. Hawkers sold peanuts, patés, spoursop juice, bananas, tamarind paste in small cups, even plates of fish and rice. *Cruzan Rum* and *Captain Morgan* bottles gleamed in the sun along the route. Everyone was happy, with or without a little alcoholic buzz. Crowds like this could not gather in any town in America without mounted police, yellow tape lines holding everyone back, and whistles blowing at pending flare-ups.

Soon flotillas of steel pans wobbled down the route, carried by spectators who came into the street and grabbed hold of part of the framework that held it together. The musicians ponged against the steel drums, the familiar rhythms bringing dancers alongside, in front of, and behind the lively ensemble.

People poured into the streets ahead of the towering mocko jumbies, the stilt walkers who leaned against second storey balconies from time to time to rest. Excited spectators lay on the steaming macadam, arms at their sides, legs close together as the jumbies lumbered over them like creatures from *War of the Worlds*. Two of them stopped and danced like inflatable air puppets, swaying, dipping and bending as though they had no joints. One extended his leg high into the air and held it, a landlocked ballet leg. He rotated, holding the leg aloft so that it leaned against his coolie hat while the crowd applauded and called for more.

The group of four gathered at Rosalie's Boutique on Strand Street, where Rosalie had stocked her fridge with cold drinks and snacks. They set up their folding chairs and donned their straw hats. Marla slathered sunscreen everywhere, including her exposed feet. Vern refused it. "No way," he said. It'll be dripping down my face in two minutes."

Rosalie and Diarra took turns manning the shop, which would do considerable business that day, especially since a cruise ship had arrived that morning in time for the festivities.

Soon the parade made its turn and wound around from King Street to Strand Street. As the crowds rushed into the streets to take their turn supporting the steel drums, people pressed closer. Children scampered to get in front where they could see, and the crowds parted to let them in.

It seemed that every tenth person who passed by knew either Rosalie or Darryl.

"You almost have as big a fan base as Rosalie," Vern said to his friend.

"I've been here nearly six years already. Remember, it's a small island. You'll know everyone, too, when you move down here."

"Just a minute," Vern said. "Who said anything about moving?"

Rosalie and Marla hid their faces. "It was just girl talk," admitted Marla. "I can dream, can't I?" She turned her face away from Vern and looked across the street. In front of a blue and white striped canopy set up for the occasion, she saw a familiar face. "Vern...."

"Are you OK?" he said. "You look like you've seen a ghost."

"There." She pointed surreptitiously, not wanting to draw attention to an outstretched arm.

He looked in the direction of the subdued point. "It can't be," he said.

They both stared at the scantily clad blonde across from them, who was not aware of the two. She was enthralled by the mocko jumbies as they came *en force* toward them. Her hands were clasped in front of her. They wondered if she was going to join the spectators who were going into the street.

Marla leaned against Rosalie and directed her focus on the woman. "Do you know her?" she asked.

Rosalie gave her a thorough going over. "I think she's new here. Darryl, do you recognize that blonde?"

207

He joined in the examination. "Yeah, she works at the casino. Blackjack dealer, I'm pretty sure."

"He would know," Rosalie said as she jerked her head toward him.

"Do you see George or Grace near her?" Vern asked Darryl.

Darryl scanned the crowd. "I don't believe I'd recognize Grace, but I don't see George anywhere."

"From what I can recall of the few pictures we've seen of Grace, I don't see anyone who looks like her," said Marla.

The woman in question caught sight of them and opened her mouth wide in an "Oh my God!" Making eye contact with Vern, she mouthed, "Vern?"

He nodded, which brought her rushing across the street.

"What are you doing here?" Pru asked. "Are you here to meet my Aunt Grace?"

"Is she here with you?" Vern asked, a worried look in his eyes as he scanned the crowd across the street. He carefully examined the expanse, the sea directly ahead, the seawall fringed with palm trees and pillars connected with heavy chains that led to the pier. There at the far end, a cruise ship sat, its passengers ringing the parade route.

"No, but I'm gonna meet her at Cheeseburger's later. What's the deal?"

"She doesn't know we're here, and I want to keep it that way," he said. He told her of the visit to Jane's, the photo of the Botanical Gardens, and most important, the need to keep it a secret. "I promised your mother I wouldn't involve her. She doesn't know I'm familiar with St. Croix and that I have good friends here."

"Always the scruples. You really are a nice guy." She looked over at Marla. Her pensive expression revealed that she still had no love for her. "Can we go somewhere quieter and talk?"

Rosalie nodded toward her shop. "Just tell Diarra you're going back to the kitchen," she said.

"Nice," said Pru. "You're friends with the owner?"

"Wow. I'm sorry for being so rude," said Vern. He introduced Pru to his friends before going indoors.

The three settled into the small kitchen area where Marla searched for Rosalie's famous chai.

"So," began Vern, "what brings you to St. Croix?"

"I never sent you an official thank you, but I put that thousand dollars in the bank and started a plan for a new life. Aunt Grace always favored me, so I decided to look her up and come down for a visit. She said that between her kids and my mom's kids, I was the one most like her."

Marla almost enthusiastically nodded in agreement, but looked at Vern first and remained impassive as she set the mugs of tea on the small folding table. She thought back at how Vern said she almost spoiled everything with her remarks at Pru's apartment and decided it was best to speak only when spoken to.

"Aunt Grace encouraged me to move here and start over," continued Pru. "She said that the island was a fresh start for her, that she was beginning to find herself." Pru stirred her tea. "One of my new *me* habits – tea without rum."

"I hope it doesn't bother you if we drink." He motioned toward a rum bottle which was poised over his cup, Marla's already having been spiked.

"No problem," she assured him.

"Did she mention the sticky little subject of me?"

"As a matter of fact, we've had several conversations about you. She knew from my mom that we had met. I really had forgotten that story of your death. That was all so long ago."

"And did she sound like she'd ever admit to her husband and kids about me?"

"Not a chance. She said she'd even visited a shrink for about six months but just couldn't do it. She really hated that you were trying to find her." She looked between the privacy curtains that separated the kitchen from the shop to the action of the parade. A scratch band on a pick-up truck was belting out salsa music, offkey trumpets dominating. The crowd was going wild, dancing alongside the truck and squealing in delight. She wiggled in her seat to the beat of the music. Her face colored as she told Vern and Marla how she'd found her niche here. "Everybody loves me," she explained.

"Do you live with Grace?" Vern asked.

"I did, in the beginning, but I found a small place out east, near the Divi Carina casino. I work there now."

"How about if we stop out there some night?" He looked at Marla for approval.

"Sure," Marla said, "I'd like to try my luck."

"Come out tomorrow night. I'll be working. There's a great band playing there. I'll sit with you during my break from six to seven."

"What time are you meeting Grace today at Cheeseburger's?" Vern asked.

"Seven."

"Do you mind if we *happen* to be there?"

"It's a public place, not to mention the best place on island for cheeseburgers." Looking over at Marla, she added, "And the best spot for margaritas. " She held her cup out as if to propose a toast to Marla. "Y'know – my episode with the two of you was not one of my best performances. On the other hand," she added, looking directly at Marla, "I think we both rattled each other's cage... That sorta brought out the worst in me. Is it possible to start over?"

"All's well that ends well has always been my mantra," said Marla. "Let's just move past it?" She returned the toast with her cup of tea. Seeing the chance to now enter the conversation, she asked, "How long have you been on St. Croix?"

"I moved down here in June. Uncle George has a lot of contacts and got me the job out at the casino. I started two weeks after I arrived."

"Funny," said Vern. "Your mom never mentioned that you moved here. Does she know?"

"Yeah, she knows, but she told me not to tell you." She laughed at the statement. "As if I kept in touch with you..." She drank the last of her chai. "I really am my Aunt Grace. The wild cannon. I told her I hadn't heard from you since your visit." Pru rocked to the music as the local high school jazz band went down the street.

"Your mom probably thought I might want to contact you and would find out that Grace lives here."

"Will you tell her of your trip here?"

211

"Yes. We're supposed to get together at Easter. I'll fill her in then."

Pru twisted her earlobe and hunched her shoulders. Leaning into the table, she said, "Maybe we'll all be a big happy family by then. I'm sure you'll win Grace over – if you ever meet her."

"If we don't see her tonight, we plan to go to the yacht club tomorrow for brunch and hope to see her there. I really don't suppose we'll actually *meet* her at either place."

*****

That night they arrived at Cheeseburger's a half hour before Grace's entourage was expected. They took a table in a corner of the open seating area where they could see patrons coming in from the parking lot. They had come alone because they were afraid George might want to come over and speak to Darryl. They knew that was a possibility at the club, too, but wanted one night where they could be anonymous voyeurs.

They arrived in separate cars. First Pru came into the seating area accompanied by a man who reminded Vern of the local character, Sharky, whom they'd met when they were on island before. He was short with dark leathery skin, arms knotted with ropey muscles, and legs bent and bowed. Compared to Pru's light complexion and blonde hair bleached both from the sun and chemicals, they looked like a Halloween pair that might be called Night and Day.

Pru silently acknowledged them and steered her partner to a table that was in clear sight of Vern and

Marla. The outdoor area featured oversized beach umbrellas scattered about in case of rain and mosquito repellent in baskets strategically placed. On the other side of the open area was an enclosed section where patrons went if rain was imminent. Most of the time the outdoor tables were fully occupied since the rain was very considerate, usually falling after operating hours.

Vern and Marla had already ordered and missed Grace and George's arrival as their nachos, burger, and fries all came at the same time. When they looked up, Grace was pulling her chair into place and talking animatedly to Pru. The four seemed familiar with each other, so they assumed the grizzled guest was not a new entity.

Vern did not touch his burger. He was spellbound by the sight of his mother. He examined her face, looking for his own features as he had at the photos he had seen at Pru's and Jane's. In person they were clearer: the carved Nordic features, a little softer on her than him due to both the feminine lines and age. Her cobalt blue eyes, though slightly dimmed, were visible even from the distance that separated them. Her graying hair pulled back in a braided bun still had strands of blond scattered throughout. He thought she had probably been an attractive young woman, more beautiful than the old photos portrayed.

'"She looks pretty good, doesn't she? That's where your good looks come from." Marla interrupted his intense stare and contemplative demeanor.

"Well, she's got that going for her." He reached for his burger and slathered it with ketchup and mustard, took a big bite, and continued watching Grace as he slowly chewed. She really doesn't look like the kind of woman who would abandon her child, he thought. She looks perfectly normal, whatever that is. Just as the picture that hung on Jane's wall, this Grace was a picture of contentedness. The way she smiled at her husband, the interchanges between her and Pru, her and the mystery man – all showed a happy, healthy woman in her sixties, possibly talking of grandchildren, past happy memories, experiences they had shared. There was nothing to indicate that the man sitting across the lot from her was the one deep dark secret she wished had never happened.

As he stared, he noticed some discomfort emanating from Grace. She began to squirm in her seat, placed her hand on her left cheek and slid it up to her eye, looked around as though she felt someone staring at her, that uncanny feeling one who is under surveillance gets. She abruptly turned toward Vern and for a long second, their eyes met. It was an electric moment. They faced off like two dogs who meet in the street. Neither wavered. She clenched her jaw and shook her head, just the slightest movement that went unnoticed by everyone except Vern. He held his gaze while she turned away from the encounter. But something had changed in her.

She seemed nervous as she spoke to the waitress who had brought armfuls of burgers and nachos, the two mainstays at the restaurant. Another waitress came with a pitcher of beer. Grace reached for her glass, which was the first to be poured. She looked over the rim as she downed the first gulp and caught Vern staring at her again. Her neck and shoulders visibly tightened the moment before the beer stuck in her throat. She coughed and excused herself from the table.

On the way back from the restroom, she glanced toward the table again. This time Vern did not watch her but resumed the surveillance when her back was turned. Instead of returning to her previous seat, she chose a chair opposite her husband, casting a sidelong glance to the offensive couple as she sat with her back to them. Although he couldn't see her facial expressions, he could tell by the way she repeatedly rolled her sleeves up and down, the way she felt around her collar, straightening it again and again, that she was annoyed. She swept her brow several times even though it was not particularly hot or humid that night, was in fact very comfortable.

Vern and Marla finished their meal and paid at the cash register. They passed far to the side of Grace's table, not looking toward the small group. Vern couldn't resist getting one more look at his mother before stepping over the railroad tie barriers that kept cars from driving into the eating area. As he turned for one last look, their eyes met again. Grace's look was one of terror as they locked again, mesmerized by each other, as though looking into a mirror.

Fran Hasson

Chapter 17

Some haunted by the ghosts they have deposed
William Shakespeare, *Richard III*

LATER THAT NIGHT Vern received a phone call from
Pru. "Quite a staring contest you two had," she said.
"She was really jittery the rest of the night. As soon as
you left, the air between her and the rest of us went
suddenly cold. We had been talking about the Three
Kings Day Parade when she blurted out, 'Who were
they?'" Pru stopped for a breath. "We all just looked at
each other. Of course I knew who she meant, but nobody
else had even noticed you."

Vern said, "So what did you say?"

"I just sat there and played dumb. George asked
who she meant, what was she talking about. And
Malcolm was just plain out of it, which is normal for
him." She told how Grace had bored into her with
accusing eyes. "Probably because I kept looking down
and avoiding her. She's pretty eerie that way, reading
minds – at least mine. She looked directly at me when

she said you looked *familiar*...She watched me rub my ear as she said this. She told me one time that I always did that when I was uncomfortable or telling a white lie."

Vern laughed at that. "I don't tell too many white lies anymore, but, as you know, I rub that same earlobe, too, whenever things get sketchy."

"I'll tell you one thing. I'm not going to the yacht club tomorrow. Can't use the hangover excuse now that I don't drink anymore, but I'll come up with something. I think the shit's gonna hit the fan when she sees you there. She'll surely notice you. I'll tell her later I couldn't say anything because George was there – which, of course, is the truth. "

"Thanks a million, Pru. I owe you."

"No, I owe you. I want to keep in touch with you – and even Marla." She chuckled a bit. "Aunt Grace will call me after brunch. If you go there with your friends, she'll sic George on them and find out who you are. Will she speak to you? Don't bank on it. If anything, check your drinks. Don't leave them unattended."

"Serious?" asked Vern.

"No, that was a joke. Grace is not a violent person. That was a bad joke. She won't be happy to know it's you. I mean how many Vern and Marla combos are there? Especially a Vern who's the spitting image of her? Who looks *familiar*...She'll make the connection, for sure."

"It'll be interesting. Maybe Marla can catch her in the women's room."

"I wouldn't recommend it."

Vern laughed at the curtness of the reply. Even though Pru had warmed up a little when it came to Marla, her tone implied she still had reservations. He wasn't sure whether Pru thought Grace was a threat to Marla or the other way around.

"By the way, cuz, was that your significant other, Malcolm?"

"God, no. He's more like my *in*significant other. He really wants to get in my pants, but you've got a much greater chance of hugs and kisses from Grace. I just give him the privilege of looking down my blouse every once in a while. That's probably all he's capable of, anyway."

Vern was enjoying his conversation with this spicy cousin, bursting out laughing at some of her frank comments. Every time he would laugh, Oliver would wag his tail and jump up at him. He rubbed the little dog's head and said to Pru, "You're a heartbreaker. Even Rosalie's dog likes you."

She said, "Malcolm keeps the other dogs at bay. I'm telling you – I've turned over a new leaf. I'm reinventing myself."

"Well, Pru, don't change too much. Just the things that are unhealthy. I really look forward to staying in touch with you."

He noticed Marla grimace when he made his parting remarks. He said to Marla, "I hope we see more of her." Her skeptical setting of the mouth, the dimpling of her cheek warned him that she did not share his feeling. "Let's give her a chance, OK?"

*****

They arrived at the yacht club around 10:30, a good time to catch Grace and George. Rosalie figured they would either go early for the opening at ten or come a little later to catch the tail end before noon. In either case, they would be there when the Elsmeres were there. As he had done at Cheeseburger's, Vern chose seats for the four of them at the far end of the room, where they could see patrons enter the covered pavilion.

The pair came in with a younger couple just as the four had received their coffee. Looking over the rim of his cup, Vern announced quietly, "Bandits at one o'clock."

They all looked toward the entrance and spotted the small group talking to the receptionist. Grace was fresh in her dotted Swiss cotton shirt and white twill Capris. Her hair was pulled back in its bun, set off by fresh-cut orange bougainvillea. She exhibited none of the anger or annoyance from the night before. Wearing a bright smile, she seemed relaxed, at ease with herself and her husband. She placed her hand on his hip pocket and leaned against his shoulder as they left the receptionist.

"She got over whatever I did to her last night," Vern said quietly to Marla.

Darryl came back with, "Still impressed with yourself, heh? Think you broke her heart?"

Rosalie gave a more-than-gentle nudge to Darryl. "I can't take you anywhere," she said.

Vern laughed it off. "Don't worry, Rosalie, nothing he says bothers me. That would be giving him too much respect."

Marla ran her hands through her hair. "It would never work – these two as business partners," she said to Rosalie.

"There you go again," said Vern. "What's going on between you guys? Who said anything about business partners?"

He and Darryl exchanged glances. Behind Darryl, Vern saw that Grace and her group were approaching a table not too far from them. Grace was joking with the younger woman until she turned her head toward Vern's table. Their eyes met again. She stopped mid-sentence and froze on the spot, mouth hanging open.

George noticed the change in her and asked, "What's the matter?"

"Straight ahead, by the restrooms – that's the couple who were at Cheeseburger's last night." She allowed George to pull her chair out and sank into it. "Do you know who they are?"

"I'll check them out when we go to the buffet."

Vern did not look her way. His group went on with their conversation, returned to the buffet for refills, and chatted with members who came over to talk to Rosalie and Darryl.

Grace continued to watch. She and George went to the buffet and filled their plates. Grace took only a few sections of grapefruit and a spoon of scrambled eggs. While at the buffet, she glanced at Vern's group from time to time to see if he was watching her. She noticed the couple he was with. "That's Rosalie McGee from the boutique," she said quietly to George on the way back to the table.

"And Darryl Fleming, the computer guy at Gallows Bay," added George. "I'll go over and talk to him. I'll find out who the mystery couple is."

"Finish your breakfast first," she said, arranging herself in her seat. "It's not that important. It can wait."

"Are you sure? They seem to rattle you."

Grace ignored him as she pushed the tiny clump of eggs around her plate and left the grapefruit untouched. She stood and walked to the cigarette machine, stashed a pack of Marlboros in her bag and returned to the table, George's troubled eyes following her.

When she returned, George said, "I know you're upset. Is it them?"

"It's nothing."

Their friends, Audrey and Steve, seemed unaware of Grace's agitation. They lingered at the buffet, choosing a mound of food, making selections from the various egg dishes, fruits, pastries, and cooked meats. On the way back, they stopped to talk to the guitarist who was making a special appearance there that morning. Turning from the entertainment podium, Steve spotted Darryl, his teammate at the Pelican Cove Team Trivia competitions. He walked over to Darryl's group as Audrey cautioned him to hurry back to the table, that their food would be ice cold. He stayed long enough for introductions and joined her.

"Hey, George, I think we have another team member for Wednesday night," announced Steve, as he emptied his tray onto the table.

Grace paled as he continued.

"Darryl's friends who are visiting the island will come and join us. His friend, Vern, was a member of his team in Delaware."

Grace pushed her chair back and stood. "I think I'm going to throw up," she mumbled and quickly sped off to the ladies' room, hand over her mouth and hunched over as she sped past Vern's table.

Fran Hasson

Chapter 18

And forgive us our trespasses as we forgive those who trespass
against us
The Lord's Prayer

VERN CALLED PRU the minute they returned from the club. It was mid-afternoon and the breeze floating through Rosalie's home refreshed him. Marla had warned him to use sunscreen, but he had declined and now the sweat beading on his forehead felt cooled by the gentle afternoon wind.

"Where have you been?" demanded Pru. "I've been calling you for hours."

"Sorry, my phone was turned off. We went out on Darryl's sailboat to Buck Island. I guess your calls must mean that Grace phoned you." He told her of the mad dash to the restroom. Being so close, they could hear the activity inside, as could other patrons. Audrey had gone into the restroom to see how Grace was doing. When Grace came out, her face green and body trembling, George had raced toward her. The maitre'd came over.

"The whole place was on her, not exactly what she wanted, I suppose."

Vern didn't tell her how he actually was amused by it all, how he almost enjoyed her distress. It was kind of like some justice being served, he had thought, as he observed Grace in her misery.

"I guess that's when they left. It's too bad they came together because they were supposed to go out on George's boat," said Pru.

"Sounds like Grace ruined everybody's day."

"She's had a reputation for doing that for many years, but I know she didn't want to do it this morning." Pru leaned close to the mirror in her tiny bathroom and finished applying her lipstick. While her little stucco house was far superior to her apartment in Vegas, the space was quite limited. She had one foot on the lip of the shower stall, raising herself higher to peer into the pitted mirror. "Look cuz, I have to go to work in about fifteen minutes, but I'm actually worried about my aunt."

"Why?"

"She was talkin' some pretty serious shit, like she didn't know what she was going to do." She balanced the phone on her shoulder as she twisted her hair into a messy braid, bright red and turquoise plastic barrettes, holding sections in place.

"What do you mean, serious shit?"

"She was crying hysterically. George had gone back out to the yacht club to pick up Audrey and Steve when she called me. I've never heard my aunt cry before."

Pru paused, as though she was re-living the sound of those cries. "When she stopped sobbing, she chewed me out because she knew I knew who you were and didn't tell her. I calmed her down a bit, told her I didn't call her this morning because I didn't want to say anything when George was around."

She straightened her uniform and checked herself in the full-length mirror at the end of the hall. "But she was sayin' crazy shit. Like *I can't go on. Who will take care of my dogs?* Stuff like that." She looked at her watch and checked her wall clock. "Look, I really have to go now."

"We'll come out to Divi tonight and talk more about this," said Vern. "Is there anything I can do in the meantime?"

"Yeah, disappear. Let it be known you're leaving the island!"

Marla had been seated on the rattan chair facing Vern during the labored conversation. She knew from his tone and the knitted brows that the encounter had been a game changer for Grace. "So what is our drama queen up to now?" she asked

He told her what Pru had said. Oliver stuffed his snout into Vern's lap as though he understood the severity of the situation, and Vern responded by hugging the dog. "From what she said, I'm afraid I've pushed Grace over the edge and she may be thinking of suicide, or at best, moving from here to escape us."

Marla moved over to him and put her arms around his shoulder, kissed him lightly on his sunburned cheek. "Whatever she decides, you didn't push her over the edge. Her demons did."

Oliver shinnied up on the chair and nudged Marla away from Vern.

They both laughed.

"Morphed Marmalade," chuckled Vern. "We need to do something, but Pru says the best thing we can do is go away."

"Do you think you can get a chance to talk to Grace when no one else is around?"

"We'll see if we can set that up when we go to Divi tonight. I just hope she didn't do anything brash while George was picking up the other couple."

Marla went inside to help Rosalie with dinner preparations. Vern sat on the verandah listening to the tree frogs and chattering birds. Oliver remained in his lap. He considered riding over to Cotton Valley and going past Grace's. Would she actually kill herself? Could he talk to her and assure her he wouldn't intrude on her life, wouldn't tell her husband? Hadn't he already intruded on her life? Was it wrong for him to have come to the island and search her out?

He thought about the stress he'd placed on Grace, tried to put himself in her shoes. It was hard for him to do that because it was still unfathomable to him that she could have spent the last thirty-seven years denying his existence. He couldn't imagine his real mother, Katherine, having led such a deceptive life. Then again, Katherine had deceived him, too, having kept his adoption such a secret for so long. No wonder she could have had such empathy for Grace. He remembered her farewell letter and her plea that he should forgive Grace. He wondered if it was a plea that he should forgive her, too. Until this moment he had never considered that she needed forgiving. His chin quivered a little. He patted Oliver's shaggy head and pulled the dog closer to his face, nuzzled him and roughed up his head. "You don't have problems like this, do you, little buddy?" he whispered into Oliver's ear.

The sun dropped below Blue Mountain in the distance, bringing on a refreshing coolness and sharpness. There were fewer shadows on the grounds and in Vern's mind. The thought of forgiveness struck him anew as the night sounds began to emerge – more frogs joined in the chorus, a lizard scampered quietly across the rail by his side, the whooshing of bats' wings skimmed by, and Oliver softly growled at the increasing activity.

Vern remembered that, in her letter, his mother had stressed how damaged Grace must be as she implored him to help heal her.

How ironic, he thought. He had come here to help heal himself, to see this woman and either make peace with her or go away forever and put her out of his mind. Instead, he had ended up driving her more into her tormented state. He had found no comfort in the mere seeing of her. What did he really want from this trip? What did he want Grace Elsmere to do?

Fran Hasson

Chapter 19

Let us affirm what seems to be the truth.
Plato, *The Republic*

GRACE LEANED HER HEAD against the window on the ride home.

"Don't you want the window down?" asked George. "The fresh air might do you some good."

"The AC feels better," she mumbled. The bougainvillea had fallen from her hair and the polka dotted top was soaked where she had washed the vomit from it.

"Your color's coming back." George kept looking over at her as he drove. He rounded the curves slowly as they made their way back to Cotton Valley, fearing the motion might trigger another episode.

"Can you go *any* slower?" Grace snapped.

He pulled over at Duggan's Reef and took a long look at his wife. "We've got a real problem here," he said.

"What does that mean?" She sat up straight, facing him squarely. "One bout of throwing up my guts is a *real problem*? It's not like it's morning sickness or something." She rummaged through her handbag and fished out a cigarette.

"I see you have your smokescreen ready. I thought you quit smoking."

Her hands shook as she lit up. She inhaled deeply, lowered the window, and blew the smoke out.

George circled around the parking lot past the chained section leading to the beach and resumed their trip home. "It seems to me," he said, "that the couple from Delaware have something to do with this."

She bit her bottom lip and looked out at the sea. She knew he was watching for her reaction. She merely took a puff of the cigarette, flicked it out, and raised the window back up. Reaching for the air conditioning fan, she said, "And now, Dr. Padereau, I presume..."

"No, Grace, I'm the man who loves you. Remember me?"

She avoided his gaze. "We need to do something about these ruts," she said as they bounced on the uneven dirt road that led to their house.

"Please don't change the subject," he said. "Can't we get to the bottom of this?"

"No."

"Is this the same issue that bothered you last year?"

"Look — I just turned myself inside out, throwing up. Did it ever occur to you I might have the flu? Maybe a bug going around? Get to the bottom of what? My stomach?" She got out of the car a second before he came to a halt under the carport. Pushing through the gate, she strode through the courtyard past the pool and stormed in the kitchen door. There, her faithful companions Tiger and Ginger whined and leaped all over her. The branches of the ornamental palm tree were still quivering when George came through the gate.

George was greeted by Juniper, the third dog of the house, the one who, like George, remained steady, never demanding attention but always there to defend and be the rational one. The dog wagged his tail and danced around George until he received his reward, a roughing up and pat on the head.

George watched Grace head for the bedroom, where she closed the door. He followed her and stood beside the bed as she changed her outfit. "Are we going to talk about this?" he asked.

"Talk, talk, talk. What *really* makes you think this is more than a bug?" She went into the hall and threw her soiled clothes into the washer, added some other items, and set the controls.

"Grace, give me some credit." He added some items from the hamper before the wash cycle started, brushing against her as she dashed back into the bedroom. "You were in a snit last night. It was obvious those two disturbed you for some reason. Then you were fine this morning until you saw them and until Steve came back from the buffet."

"Give it a break, George. Don't you have to go back to the club and take Steve and Audrey out on the boat?" She thought about it for a minute and wondered if he would ask for more information about Vern once he got there, if Vern would still be there.

But George seemed to have had enough of her evasiveness and took the bait. Before she could reverse field, he stood in the bedroom doorway and almost snarling at her, wheeled around. She heard him mutter, "I'm sick and tired of being vacuumed into your dysfunction."

She went into the hall to stop him; however, she heard him close the French doors in the kitchen with an uncustomary bang. She raced to the doorway, ready to call out as he threw his hand up against the lowhanging branches of the palm tree and set it waving again when he opened the gate. He quickly set the car into reverse and backed out of the carport, creating a whorl of dust as he sped down the dirt road.

She thought it strange that he had taken her car instead of his. He would never drive it because it had no seat belts and no airbag. He's really pissed, she thought. He was always bugging her to get rid of the Explorer and buy a *real* car. He seemed hellbent on getting there as fast as possible, and while her "island car" was lacking some essentials, it was much faster than his airconditioned two-cylinder Fiat.

She hoped Vern and his party had left before he got back to the club. She went to the phone and pushed the speed dial for Pru. Nervously rifling through a stack of papers on the phone table, she came across a business card for Darryl's shop. Pru answered the phone just as she picked the card up. Grace launched into her tirade before Pru could finish saying hello. "Did you tell them I live here?" Her face reddened as she yelled into the phone.

"What? Wait."

"Don't what wait me. You know damn well what I'm talking about. Why didn't you tell me last night when I asked about them?" She paced back and forth from the verandah to the kitchen to the bedroom where she found her cigarettes in her purse. "How did they know I live here?" she demanded. She sat in the chair at the computer next to the phone dock and choked back sobs as she teetered toward hysteria. "How could you? My life is ruined now." Her shoulders heaved as she sobbed uncontrollably. "How could you? After all the conversations we had about him? I don't know what I'm going to do."

"Calm down, Aunt Grace. You sound like you're going to have a stroke or something. I didn't tell you last night because Uncle George was there and I'm sure you didn't want him to know. What's going on, anyway? Why are you upset this morning? How did you find out it was Vern?"

Grace took in long drags and blew out clouds of smoke. Tiger jumped up and down, clawing at her. She regained her composure while she told her about the brunch at the club.

"You're back pretty early. What time did you go out there?" After getting a clearer picture of what had happened at the yacht club, Pru tried to assure her that Vern wouldn't blow her cover. She didn't tell her that she had seen him at the parade. "If he wanted to let you know who he was, he would have said something last night at Cheeseburger's. My mother told me he is really a gentleman, not a troublemaker, and I believe that."

She reminded Grace about Vern's trip to Vegas and the thousand dollars, how her mother had befriended him and how they had talked about possibly meeting Grace one day. He assured her mother he would never do anything that would cause harm to anyone in the family. "That includes you, George, and your kids. Don't worry. He won't say anything unless you want to admit that he's your son."

"What's he doing here? You must have talked to him."

"Why do you say that?"

"Come on, Pru. How stupid do you think I am. You mean you sat there last night and never said a word to him and then acted so dumb when I asked who they were?" Grace's eyes darkened and she brushed Tiger aside as she resumed her pacing.

"All right – I had a few words with them before you came. I was surprised to find them here. And they were surprised I was here, too. My mom never told them I'd moved to St. Croix."

"So why are they here, if not to find me?"

"Those people you said they were with this morning – they're good friends. Vern used to work with that guy, Darryl. They met Rosalie here five or six years ago. Apparently Darryl's hooked up with Rosalie."

"The way he looked at me – he was staring. Like he recognized me." She turned Darryl's business card over and over. "Is it possible that it's all a coincidence? Did you tell him I was here when you talked to him last night?"

Pru was silent.

"You did!" Tears gushed now. Grace went to the rail and looked down into the valley. Through her sobs, she said, "I wish I could jump from this rail and end it all, now and forever." Looking down at her bewildered dogs, who were whining and licking at her; she reached down to pet them. "Who will love my Tiger and Ginger the way I do?"

"Aunt Grace, please – get a grip. I'll come right over. Please, you're scaring me."

"Don't come. I'll work this out." She plopped herself down on the sofa where Tiger nestled up around her neck and Ginger plastered herself to her side.

"Shall I call Uncle George on his cell? You shouldn't be alone right now."

"I'll be all right." Her sobs had tapered off to sniffles. "I need to think. Don't worry."

Fran Hasson

Chapter 20

We must not pretend to understand the world only by the intellect; we
apprehend it just as much by the feeling.
Carl Gustav Jung, *Psychological Types*

VERN AND MARLA DROVE out to the casino that
night. They ascended the wide dual staircase from the
right side. The building itself was reminiscent of
Monticello with its pillars and domed top. She leaned
against Vern on the way up and pointed to the blinking
O in the flashing CASINO sign.

"That reminds me of your mother," she said.

"You have the weirdest memories of my mother,"
Vern said, thinking back of the Naked Farmer sign.
"What now?"

"Remember how the lights blinked in her hospital
room? Maybe she's with us now." She hesitated and
added, "She said she would be."

It was a comforting thought to Vern that Katherine
could be with them. It reassured him that, no matter how
this ended, he meant no harm. It wasn't really so wrong

that he should be curious and pursue this to his fullest now that he had earnestly resumed the search. In fact, Katherine wanted him to. It occurred to him that he wanted to *help* his birth mother.

Funny, he thought, that he had come so far. That it was no longer just curiosity, a desire to make Grace want to know him, or to make himself be a more complete person but that he actually did want to bring some comfort to this woman who had so vehemently denied him.

He thought of how they had helped Pru turn her life around. All it took in that case was money and perhaps forcing her to take a good look at her life. Grace was a much harder nut to crack.

Vern began to see himself in a new light. In a way, he was prouder of himself than he had ever been, although self-esteem had never been an issue until he discovered Grace's rejection. He was beginning to internalize, to truly understand, that the fault lay with this strange mother, not him.

He remembered Katherine assuring him from her hospital bed as she unfolded the story of his adoption that he was not to blame for the rejection, that his birth mother was the one with the problem. "Funny how it's taken me to this moment in time," he said to the unsuspecting Marla, "to let that sink in."

"That she's still with us?" she asked.

At the top of the steps, he turned and took Marla's hand. They looked down at the parking lot, across the street to the Divi Carina Hotel and beyond to the dark, sea dappled by the light of the full moon.

"No. I never doubted that, but I was just remembering something she had said about Grace that I never fully believed until now."

"What*ever* are you talking about?"

He explained his *aha* moment as they continued through the entrance where they were politely welcomed by two security guards. "Remember the letter my mother left in the recipe box? How she said Grace may have led a tortured life all these years? How she said maybe I could actually help to heal her? Well... I realize now that it hasn't been enough just to see her. Maybe it won't be enough to speak to her. I truly want to help her get over all those years she's denied me."

They strolled farther from the entrance doors. "I want her to know I forgive her. I think she needs to forgive herself."

"You could be right. We've said a few times how – in her pictures - she looks like she's been happy all these years, but she wasn't the picture of happy at the club."

"I hope this trip hasn't been wasted. I hope I get the chance to talk to her." He looked around the casino. "Pru is our key to unlock the door to Grace. Funny how this has developed."

They hesitated at the edge of the circular water fountain. From there they surveyed the interior of the casino. "Beautiful marble," said Marla as she leaned against the edge of the water display, "but it needs an artistic touch to make it a little more inviting. These spouts don't do much for me."

"Maybe this could be your business when we relocate here," he said. He arched a brow and bored his laughing eyes into hers. "Did you and Rosalie actually talk about us moving here?"

"Hmmm, where do you suppose we'll find Pru?" she asked, focusing on anything other than Vern. The oval in the middle of the casino was lined with blackjack and other gaming tables, surrounded on both sides by slot machines.

"I detect a little evasion," he said with a grin. "But I'll grill you later on it." He scanned the tables for his cousin. All the dealers were dressed in black or dark blue shirts and pants.

"This doesn't look like a suitable place for Pru," Marla remarked. "I expected exotic tropical shirts with very short skirts like the waitresses are wearing."

"Remember? We're giving her a second chance."

"No, *you* are," she countered. She was the first to spot Pru. Their eyes met and Pru stood straighter, holding her head high, and motioning with a nod for them to come to her table. "Well, maybe, you're right," Marla admitted. "She seems to have come a long way."

They arranged to meet Pru in an hour at the entertainment area. "That'll give you a little time to gamble and some time to listen to the music," she told them.

Her relief dealer tapped her out, and Pru joined them at the Show Bar. Vern thought how different the tension level was at this casino meeting. This time there was a different anxiety, this one more urgent. He and Marla had both been on edge wondering who the strange Pru was over a year ago, how she fit into their search for his mother, if she really was his cousin. This time, the re-born cousin was no conundrum; it was a relief to know she was on their side, that she had begun to step back into a real world.

Fortunately the band was on break, too, and there was a temporary lull until a DJ would take the stage. "I know I wanted a quiet place to talk, but I have to admit I was enjoying the Xpress Band. Lots of island flavor," Vern said. He watched the action on the stage as the crew set up amplifiers, sound mixers, combo players, and mikes. Turning to Pru, he said, "So what do you know about Grace? Any new word since you talked this morning?"

"As a matter of fact, I called her from here the minute I arrived."

Vern let out a huge breath. "Good. She didn't put a gun to her head."

"Aunt Grace doesn't like pain. She'd never go out that way," laughed Pru. She watched the DJ check the wires and position the gear to his liking. Leaning forward, she said, "In a few minutes, that noise will blast us right out of our seats, so I'll talk fast." She told them how Grace had calmed down. George was outside cleaning out his car at the time when she briefly told Pru what she wanted of Vern. "She asked that you and Marla not go to the Team Trivia night. She wanted to calm George down and think about what to do – without the added pressure of you sitting there and staring at her ... *her* words."

"And – just go away? Not deal with it?" He twisted his earlobe. "Not deal with *me*?"

"Here's the surprising thing." Pru leaned close to Vern, Marla leaning into him at the same time. The two watched Pru like a pair of hungry wolves. "She wants to think about meeting you alone!"

Chapter 21

...for the true discoverers are among them, as comets amongst the stars.
Benjamin Daydon Jones, from *biography of Linnaeus*

GRACE SAT ON THE CHAISE LOUNGE next to her pool. A bright moon hung over Buck Island, stars adding to its luster in the dark sky. She thought it looked like something from Fantasyland the way the stars throbbed out their brilliance, the way the man in the moon smiled playfully at her, the way the tree frogs and creatures of the night skittered and tacked along the branches, across the flagstones, all working in harmony. It was a composition she had grown to love, the sounds of the island at night. Coupled with the visual images, it was better than any Academy Award winning film. The added feature it had that the films didn't share was the fragrance she inhaled from her frangipani and the night-blooming cereus and jasmine. She was not just a spectator; she was part of this scenario.

She imagined having Vern sitting next to her. He was a handsome young man in the tradition of the Seaman family but with the added coloring and bearing of her lineage. It was too bad she hadn't gotten to know Bert's brothers better. If they hadn't been killed in the crash, maybe one of them would have married her and helped raise the baby. So many what if's.... But then she would never have met George, would never have given birth to the three children she loved so dearly.

What would happen if she came clean now? Would her children think she was a monster for having given Vern up? It wasn't just the adoption – the story she had made up about his death. Would they consider everything she had worked for her whole life to have been a lie?

Could she change? She knew she had not been an easy person to live with. Her outer shell had hardened over many years. To put a chink in it now – what would that mean? Would she turn into a sniveling, little pushover? How could she expose herself now? These thoughts had come to her in sickening waves since the phone call that day when Jane first told her Vern was looking for her. She had always feared the day would come, had fretted over it for years, not with the constancy that dogged her now but with occasional bouts of dread. For the past eighteen months, this dilemma plagued her. Vern had dropped the pursuit for nearly a year, giving her a little hope that he'd go away, but now here he was, right on St. Croix. Now she had to do something.

She heard George come onto the patio, Tiger bouncing behind him. He took her elbow as he stopped next to her. "Grace, look at that falling star!"

She knew it was useless to spot a falling star someone else was lucky enough to have sighted, but she turned anyway, looking toward the sea. She sat bolt upright, dropped her mouth wide open as the meteor crossed the valley and continued on its way past Buck Island, finally disappearing. The incident lasted nearly five seconds, a lifetime when it comes to watching a falling star. Its blazing tail was brighter than anything she'd ever seen.

Speechless, they looked at each other. George sat on the end of the lounge chair as Grace settled herself back onto it, arranging Tiger on her lap. "Eerie, wasn't it?" she said.

"Something like that."

"Almost spiritual," she added.

"Funny, I was thinking the same thing." George pressed his lips together, then took in a deep breath. "Maybe it's a sign."

"Of what?"

"A new beginning."

"What does that mean?" She pulled Tiger to her chest. She wanted to say, "Bullshit," but decided she had driven George to an edge today that had not been reached before.

"I think you know. In case you don't, let me spell something out." He stood and walked to the low cinder block wall facing the valley. Looking toward the path the meteor had taken, he said, "I want to know about the couple. I want to know what they have to do with your distress." He turned to face her. "And don't tell me it's nothing."

"And if I don't tell you?"

"I'm prepared to pack my bags and move onto the boat until I find somewhere else to go."

Grace wondered if he'd heard anything at the club when he went back to pick up Steve and Audrey. They hadn't spoken about it since he came back. They'd fallen into their normal routines, George working around the house, she tending to her plants, both of them ignoring the issue. The only time they had talked at all was over dinner, a light meal. George had grilled pork chops and Grace had thrown together a salad. After that, they watched a little TV, the silence over the incident at the club pressing down on the two of them. But they sidestepped it and Grace was pleased with that.

She looked toward the heavens and played the tune in her head: *When you wish upon a star, Makes no difference who you are, Anything your heart desires Will come to you...*" She found the North Star and wished upon it that she could have a heart attack and die right on the spot. But, of course, that would be too easy.

"How much time are you giving me before your moving-out date?"

"You act like this is a joke."

"No, seriously, I need to think about it."

He sat on the lounge with her again and leaned forward. "Do you mean so you can make up a lie? Why can't you just tell me now?"

"I've been thinking all day of a way to tell you, but I need to do something first. How much time do I have?"

"They're coming to Team Trivia Wednesday night. If you haven't told me by then, I'm going to ask them if they know you. I'll have my bags in the car and will go from Pelican Cove to the boat that night."

"I want to watch the night sky for more signs," she said, an undertone of sarcasm seeping through. She turned away from him. "Is there anything else?"

He put his hands up in surrender and rose, backing away from her. "I love you, Grace, but at this point I really don't think I'm important to you or that *you* love *me*." With that he went into the house.

She sat alone, hugging her little dog with such a troubled intensity that Tiger whined to be let down. Grace mulled over the thought that George could think he was unimportant or that she didn't love him. He was the only man she had ever loved. His kindness, strength, and dependability had been her source of stability since the day she first met him, ten years after she had let Vern go. Other men had come in and out of her life, but she knew the moment they met at Baltimore's Inner Harbor that he was completely different from all the others.

She knew if she had told him then that he would have understood. But she had buried Vern so deeply, had worked so hard to forget him, had been so dismayed when the other men rejected her once they found out she had a child, that she couldn't put him to the test. No, George Elsmere was a keeper.

Two days. She had two days to figure it out, to save her marriage. She searched the sky again for a sign. "Are you there, God?" she whispered. "Can you tell me what to do?"

It came to her that she and Pru had discussed the possibility earlier about a meeting. It was only rhetorical then. She would call Pru as soon as George left the house the next morning and arrange a meeting with Vern at Pru's place. There was so much to consider.

Chapter 22

Serene, I fold my hands and wait
John Burroughs, *Waiting*

PRU RAN AROUND straightening her tiny home. She shook the throw that hid the stains on her sofa, straightened the faded tropical prints in the living room, and dusted the frame of her Las Vegas painting. She washed the remaining dishes from last night's snack and her morning coffee and bun. Then she put the coffee grounds in the compost pile at the back of her yard before she swept the sand from the entrance to her kitchen.

She was quite proud of her two bedroom house on the knoll overlooking the casino where she worked. She liked that the kitchen door was the main entrance. She always felt most at home in that room of anyone's house, remembering the days when she was young. So much was learned at the dinner table, the center of activity. She was the center of the activity now with the looming meeting between Vern and his mother; how

251

appropriate that they would be entering through her kitchen.

Grace was to arrive at ten and Vern and Marla a half hour later. Grace insisted on being there before the pair to settle her nerves, to watch them approach, to steel herself against any emotional outburst. Was she supposed to throw herself at their feet, grasp them in a group bear hug, seat herself and have them bow down before her? Pru tried to assure her that she could be any way she wanted to be. She said Vern had no requirements. He was overjoyed that she had agreed to the meeting. "He'll do whatever you say," she had told Grace on the phone.

"And if I tell him not to go to Team Trivia, not to show his face again on the island before leaving, not to come back again – will he do all those things?'

"Aunt Grace – they have friends here. Of course he won't agree to never come again. But I'm pretty sure he'll do the other two."

She set the pot of water for tea on the stovetop and readied the coffee maker so she needed only to push the ON button, arranged pastries on her yellow plastic serving platter, and set the table with four mismatched plastic cups and saucers. When her cat jumped up on the table, she shooed him away and quickly covered the pastry plate with plastic wrap. Next she began to pace. If she hadn't given up alcohol, this would have been the point where she'd have fixed a tumbler for herself.

Ten o'clock passed and no Aunt Grace. Pru stood in the doorway and peered down South Shore Road. No cars were on the road for as far as she could see. Grace would have come from East End Road and merged onto

South Shore. From her vantage point, she could see from Grapetree Bay all the way to Isaac's Bay. No cars were visible.

Vern and Marla would be arriving from the opposite direction, would drive almost to the hotel and casino before reaching her bright blue stucco house. When she looked to her left, she didn't see any cars heading toward her from there, either. Ten twenty. She called Grace. There was no answer. It was hard to believe Grace did not carry a cell phone. The fact that she wasn't answering her home phone was a good sign. Or was it? She must be on her way here, Pru thought.

She tried to busy herself dusting the end tables by her bed, straightening her blankets and re-fluffing the pillows. When she heard car tires coming up the gravel road, she breathed a sigh of relief. She expected to see Grace racing to the door, red in the face, her hair flowing out of her usual tightly woven bun. Instead she saw Vern and Marla parking next to her Jeep. She checked her watch – ten thirty-five.

She watched as Vern unfolded his long frame from the Mazda convertible. She laughed at the effort he was making and called out, "Why didn't you just climb over the door – looks like that'd be easier."

Vern and Marla looked out to the highway. "Is Grace here yet?" he asked.

"No. I called her house but got no answer." She looked toward Grace's route and still seeing no cars, said, "C'mon in. I'll try her number again."

"Maybe she chickened out," said Vern. He looked down at his hands and shook his head.

Marla reached out to hold his hand. "Maybe she had a flat tire, or maybe her car wouldn't start."

Pru countered that with, "She'd have called from home if she couldn't get the car started." She stood in the doorway, pushed speed dial on her phone and craned to see as far as possible. "I'm worried."

Still no answer.

Vern's voice shook. "Shall we go to her house and see if she's OK, or call her husband and see if he can go check?"

"Uncle George is at the club. He'll be on a job until the afternoon. Let's give her until eleven."

"Then what?" asked Marla.

"Then we'll drive over to her house along the route she'd take to get here."

Chapter 23

We do earnestly repent,
And are sorry for these, our misdoings
The Book of Common Prayer
The General Confession

GRACE WOUND HER BRAIDED BUN into a tight knot. She laced a few strands of red bougainvillea into the braid to match the red Capris and white linen blouse she wore. She gave Tiger and Ginger pats and hugs before closing them onto the verandah. "Sorry, my sweets, but I'll be gone for a couple hours, so you're banished."

As she stepped into her Explorer, she looked over to where they were scratching at the wire that enclosed the parts they could reach. They had gone through the rails too many times and chased her down the rutted road, making her return to put them in the house. George had installed the wire so they couldn't slip through.

She paled as she thought back to her considering suicide. Her two furry loves were what kept her from seriously taking steps to end her life. They depended on her. She loved them in a way she felt no one else would. She liked George's dog, Juniper, well enough, but he was George's dog, not hers. Her two adored her and she returned that love to them. She could never leave them. She could imagine them whining, sniffing her shoes, rummaging through the bedsheets, watching from the verandah, waiting for her return. She couldn't do that to them.

This line of thinking made her grip the wheel tighter. *Them*? What about George? What about her children? Her sister? Vern? Would she place the burden on Vern of being the reason for her suicide? Did she dread so much meeting him and revealing herself that she would choose suicide rather than owning up to the abandonment?

Did George really love her like he said he did? If so, how could he have threatened to leave her? He'd get along without her. Her children were adults, managing on their own. Her sister had a network of family to support her.

In the final analysis, her death would affect her Tiger and Ginger more than anyone else. Even Vern – was he really so sensitive that he'd hold himself responsible for her death? From all accounts, he was conscientious. Hadn't he kept the secret from George? Hadn't he declined to push the issue of meeting her and her children? He'd survive.

She ran over the script she had prepared for the meeting. She would ask Vern to leave the island without seeing George. Then she would confess to George tonight after she and Vern had straightened everything out. She would ask Vern to keep her secret until after she'd died. Then he could meet her other children. She would never see him again. Black and white. The end of it.

If he were to return to St. Croix, she would ignore him. No phone calls, no Christmas cards, birthday cards, visits back and forth. She was meeting him merely to satisfy his curiosity. If he had questions about family health conditions, his grandparents, or other such concerns, surely he could get that information from his Aunt Jane, whom he had befriended.

As far as his paternal side of the family, she would not divulge that. She could never admit to that night, and the Seaman brothers were not there to tell that tale. As far as she knew, they'd never told anyone of their behavior. They would have suffered as much from the embarrassment as she would. The family would have held them every bit as responsible as she. She would not tell Vern who his father was or who he could have been.

She made the turn onto South Shore Road and was admiring the view of Grapetree Bay, the white sand, brilliant cerulean sea, the color pumped brighter by the clear sky and puffs of floating white clouds. A palm tree here and there shading the elegant, landscaped mansions along the stretch provided a perfect foreground to this masterpiece. What a beautiful island. Her home. George's home. A place where she had finally found some measure of peace. Settling with Vern would certify this new lease on life.

Her right arm tingled. She looked down and froze. A small brown spider scrabbled toward her hand. She immediately spotted the violin shape on its upper body and tried to shake it off her arm. She let go of the wheel with her left hand and batted at it. The brown recluse spider, angered and afraid, bit deeply before being cast aside.

The car swerved to the right, then the left, then plowed into a pathway that led to the sea. Grace's fear was driving the car. She floored the gas pedal instead of the brakes and rammed through tall bush, crashed into a concrete land marker, and came to a sudden, jerking halt. Her head slammed against the windshield, shattering the safety glass and knocking her unconscious.

A trade wind blew through the ravaged auto, cooling her blood as it coagulated on her forehead, drying the sweat that had accompanied the heat and shock. She lay there, her braid coated with blood, the flowers wilting, her life waning.

She awoke to severe pain in her head and arm. She opened her eyes slowly and tried to focus. Where was she? What happened? Her right arm was swollen to the size of her thigh. She couldn't lift it. She tried to open the door, but it was held fast, pinned against the concrete. She was in the middle of a copse of sea grass on one side, the marker that served as a property line on one side, and a small clearing that revealed the sea in front of her. She couldn't turn to see what was behind. Grace knew she had lost too much blood. She felt the sticky mass on her head, saw the linen blouse soaked through to her skin.

She remembered the spider and knew the swelling on her arm was the result of the bite. She knew if she was allergic, as she was to bees, that medical care was urgent. But she couldn't move. Besides the door being jammed, she was wedged tight by the steering wheel.

Her life passed before her eyes, the way they always said in stories that it did. George, her kids – all four of them, Tiger and Ginger. Shit, she thought, is this how it's going to end? She dabbed her left index finger into the blood on her shirt and scrawled on her swollen right arm, *I'm sorry*.

Her world turned black again.

Fran Hasson

Chapter 24

...he is alone, abandoned on earth in the midst of his infinite
responsibilities, without help...
Jean Paul Sartre
Being and Nothingness

"WE'LL TAKE MY JEEP," Pru said.

They started out at a few minutes past eleven and backtracked down South Shore Road to where it merged with East End Road and on to Cotton Valley. When they reached Cotton Valley Trail, Marla spotted a green Datsun parked on the side. "Is that her?" she called.

"No," said Pru. "She has a burgundy Explorer, looks like a battering ram. Bought it for about two hundred dollars." She rolled her eyes at the thought of the "island car," as Grace called it. "At least it didn't break down on the way or we'd have passed it."

"How in the hell does anyone drive this road day in and day out?" Vern asked as they bounced and jounced up the road to Grace's house.

Pru merely laughed.

They could hear the dogs before they saw the house. Pulling into the carport, Pru said, "Those are her faithful watchdogs." They could see Tiger and Ginger throwing themselves against the rails in a futile attempt to break free. "Be back later, kids!" she called to the dogs before backing out and heading back the way they'd come.

"What now?" Vern asked.

"Let's check the roads more carefully going back, look for any turn-offs where she might have pulled over. Maybe we missed her sitting by the car waiting for help to arrive." Pru twisted her earlobe and wiped her brow. "Uncle George hates that car. He also hates that she won't carry a cell phone."

They pulled into Ziggy's and called the owner over.

"Hiya, Pru," he said. "What brings you over this way? That ornery aunt of yours?" He looked into the Jeep, obviously waiting for an introduction.

"As a matter of fact, yes," she answered. "Aunt Grace was supposed to come to my place and meet my guests from the States." She made the polite introductions. "Have you seen her this morning?"

"It's funny. I saw them both this morning. George came in the early shift for gas and a sandwich, and Grace stopped a while ago and filled her tank."

"Did you see which way she went?"

He pointed to the way she would have driven to go to Pru's. "I remember thinking, Why didn't she just go with George earlier?"

A half hour later, after having checked eight different breaks along the side of the road, Vern spotted an irregular pattern of bent grasses along South Shore Road. "Over there," he said. "Looks like a little trail."

"That leads to the beach," Pru said. She pulled in. They followed a pattern of erratic tire tracks and twisted foliage.

Vern swallowed. He pulled the bottom of his cargo shorts down as far as he could, smoothed them, and pulled them again. "I don't like the looks of this."

Marla spotted the Explorer first. "Over there!"

Vern was out of the Jeep before it stopped. He raced to the driver's side but couldn't squeeze between the post and the door. He ran over to the passenger side, thrashed the sea grass away from the side, and pulled the door open. "Jesus Christ! Call 911!"

He climbed into the car and reached toward the still figure. "No. Grace. No."

Marla and Pru reached the passenger side. "Is she alive?" Marla's voice trembled as did her body.

"No." After gently closing her eyelids, he slumped into the passenger seat. He stroked her hair at the nape of her neck, where the blood hadn't reached. He looked at her face. In repose, the hardness was gone. He wanted to hug her, to breathe life back into her. "Now I'll never get to know you," he whispered. As he scanned her lifeless body, he spotted the bloody message. "Look what she wrote on her arm," he said as he backed out of the car.

Marla and Pru peered inside the car while Vern put his hands on the back door and leaned against the frame. He hung his head down, his body shook, and he gasped for breath. "I told you I wouldn't run off" – Katherine's last words and "I'm sorry" – Grace's *only* words pinged through his brain. His world was collapsing.

263

Marla went to him. She held him tight, trying to soothe the trembling.

"This is all my fault," he blurted. "I shouldn't have come here. I shouldn't have pushed her into this."

"Into what?" asked Pru, who had joined them. Tears streaked her face. She wiped them aside, composed herself, and asked, "You think you caused this accident?"

He lifted his head and motioned toward Grace's body. "You really think this was an accident?"

"Oh, Vern." Pru stepped back and put her hand to her mouth. "Please, Vern. Don't do this to yourself."

"She's right," Marla said. "Grace was a smart woman. If she wanted to commit suicide, it wouldn't have been by driving into the bush. You can't blame yourself for this."

They heard the wailing of an ambulance. Pru ran out to the road and flagged the vehicle down.

Chapter 25

They spoke, I think, of perils past
They spoke, I think, of peace at last
Vachel Lindsay
The Chinese Nightingale

PRU ACTED AS THE GO-BETWEEN, informing
George first of the accident and then of Vern and
Marla's identity. George reeled at the news of her death.
"It can't be possible," he said when Pru came to the
yacht club that day. He thought of his threat to leave her.
"I pushed her into this."

When she told him of Vern and Marla, he sat down
on the dock, thrust his head into his hands. She told him
that Grace had been on her way to meet them, to finally
admit she had this long lost son. She told him she was
going to confess that evening, that her conscience was
finally going to be cleansed. "Uncle George, you didn't
push her into anything. This has bothered her for years.
She finally got the courage to do it." She squatted next to
him and hugged him as she said, "She loved you so
much. That's what gave her that courage."

265

George sobbed into his hands. "Why couldn't she tell me? I could have handled it." His body heaved and wracked. There was nothing Pru could do but watch and wait. "Are they still here? Did he threaten her? Was he blackmailing her?" His anger was beginning to rise, momentarily supplanting the grief.

"Please, Uncle George. It wasn't like that." She explained the situation and that Vern had promised not to reveal himself, that he merely wanted to meet her and talk to her.

George seemed to accept that. "I knew something was bothering her. Did this all start about a year ago?"

Pru filled him in on as much as she could before driving him to the scene of the accident. By the time they reached the spot, the rescue workers had removed Grace from the car and had taken her away. They were hooking the car to the tow truck. She told him what Grace had scrawled on her arm.

"I don't believe I ever heard Grace say I'm sorry. Maybe she finally found peace." He walked around the crash site, then disconsolately returned to Pru's car. "Will you drive me to the hospital? They'll probably want me to identify her." He sat in the car with his head in his hands and wept uncontrollably.

The days that followed were incredibly sad. George was bereft. He was surrounded by his family. The three children arrived from the States, shocked and grief-stricken. They were camped out in George and Grace's home, while some of Aunt Jane's family stayed in Pru's tiny house. Friends from the yacht club, Ziggy's, Team Trivia, and from all over the island sent condolences.

Some made their way up the rutted road to comfort George.

His usual easygoing manner was punctuated by a crestfallen attitude. The graying at his temples spread over his face, his movements slowed, and his voice cracked as he greeted mourners who stopped by the house. His children ran the house, prepared the meals, cared for the dogs. The cousins talked quietly to each other and Aunt Jane looked through Grace's books and photo albums. She spoke to George of Vern, careful to avoid such conversations when his children were in the house. She had also asked her children not to tell their cousins of Vern.

Grace's dogs searched for her, running to the door whenever a car came up the dirt road. Tiger burrowed into the sofa and tried to crawl into the pillow Grace had always rested against. Both dogs refused to eat. Their tails hung as they walked. Aunt Jane asked if she could take them back to Maryland with her since they seemed to relish the familial scent. They slept on the sofa with Jane each night, their noses inside Grace's boat shoes or her flipflops and their paws wrapped around them.

*****

Vern could not be consoled. Unable to go to Grace's house, his grief had to be suppressed, to be shared only with Marla, Rosalie, and Darryl. He paced back and forth on the verandah, shaking his head, looking to the heavens for an answer. Why did this happen? What were her last thoughts? Was she going to explain why she abandoned him? Did she ever regret it? Would they have had a future together?

Pru was the mediator. She set up a meeting at her house with George when her brother and sisters were on a trip with George's children. They were not aware of Vern's presence on the island, although her mother was.

Vern didn't know whether he should attend the funeral, whether or not he could grieve with the family, whether or not he should just return to Delaware without saying anything. Would he get the chance to see Aunt Jane, the cousins? He was relieved when George agreed to meet him.

They came face to face at Pru's house. Vern and Marla were there when George pulled into the drive. He entered through the kitchen where he was met by Pru, who led him to the living room. Vern stood, reaching out to shake hands with George. George stiffened and Vern withdrew his hand.

"I can't tell you how sorry I am for your loss," Vern said, almost in a whisper. "Thank you for agreeing to see me." He sat next to Marla. She took his hand in both of hers.

George looked around at Pru's paintings, her books, her picture albums. Everywhere but at Vern. Finally he directed his gaze at Vern. He stared intently at him causing Vern to roll his shoulders and flush slightly.

"You look like Grace," he finally said.

Vern nodded.

"I suppose you'll want to meet our children."

"That's up to you. I would have done whatever Grace wanted me to do, and now I'll do what you want."

"Certainly I want you to meet them. If they knew about you, they'd want to meet you, too." He took a deep breath and settled onto the recliner that Pru had purchased with the proceeds of the sale of her favorite Vegas chair. "But I'm not sure this is the proper time. I'm not sure it's right to have you at the funeral or to tell my kids about you. Grace's death has us all pretty torn up." He bent forward and covered his face. "This is all so sudden. I'd like some time before telling them about you."

"I respect your wishes. If you never want to tell them, I will never try to find them. I wish I hadn't tried to find Grace."

George looked directly at Vern. "You shouldn't feel that way. Grace has been running away from you for years, and I think it was a good thing that she was finally confronting her fear. She never told me about you but I'm beginning to see what's been picking at her for so long. I'm not sure who the *I'm sorry* was intended for – you for having given you up, me for keeping me in the dark, to her dogs for leaving them, to Pru for involving her ..." He couldn't go on for a long minute. "Or maybe even to God. Maybe she was asking for forgiveness from God Almighty."

George stood. He paced through the room, holding his hand on his forehead. "The autopsy said she died from blood loss and internal injuries. I wonder if fright and guilt played a part. They said she had suffered a bite from a spider, most likely a brown recluse. She was scared to death of spiders and cockroaches. That's probably why she ran off the road."

Fran Hasson

Before he left, George shook hands with Vern and told him he'd be in contact with him when things settled down. "I don't know what I'll do without her. We had some rocky times, for sure, but I loved that woman as much as a man could love any woman."

*****

Arrangements were made for Grace's funeral. She would be cremated and the cremains would be distributed in keepsake hearts like the one Marla had of her mother's ashes. They decided to reserve some and put them in an urn with Tiger and Ginger's ashes when the two dogs would die and bury them in the plot of ground by her frangipani tree. The rest would be scattered in the sea from their catamaran. "St. Croix is where Grace wanted to end her days," George said. And half-jokingly but knowing it was all too true, he added, "I sometimes thought she loved those dogs more than anybody or anything."

*****

Vern and Marla boarded their plane as the funeral procession was heading toward the yacht club. From there, the family would conduct a burial at sea with the apportioned ashes. Vern slid his titanium keepsake heart into his laptop case. "We'll put this on the shrine next to our mothers' ashes?" He looked at Marla for approval.

"You know we will."

It gave him a degree of comfort to know Katherine and Grace would be resting next to each other, that

Katherine would have liked that. But he knew, as he leaned back in his seat, he would always carry a scar that he would open and re-open whenever he played the *I'm sorry* scene back in his head, her last words etched in blood forever on his heart.

Although he was sorry that he had never made peace with Grace, he truly believed that in her final moments, she had made peace with someone, her God, perhaps, and that gave him solace. He knew he could go on without the emptiness he had been feeling. He felt sure George would keep his word and someday he would meet his siblings, that this would also ease his pain.

Lulled to sleep by the droning of the plane's engines, Vern smiled as his dream world took over. In it, Katherine, Grace, and Marla's mother, Theresa, craned to see each other on the shelf that served as a shrine in their bedroom. "Howdy, stranger," called Theresa. The other two looked back at her and Grace snapped, "Who are *you* - calling *me* strange?" Katherine merely shook her head.

THE END

Fran Hasson

Mothers and Other Strangers

Fran Hasson

8850600R00158

Printed in Great Britain
by Amazon.co.uk, Ltd.,
Marston Gate.